BECOMING A DIRECTOR?
WHAT YOU NEED TO KNOW

GW00370772

ISBN 0 86349 109 X

© Deloitte Haskins & Sells, UK. June 1988.
Produced by City Response Limited/Typesetting by Yellow Book Limited
Printed in England by Billing & Sons Ltd, Worcester

CONTENTS

Chapter   *Page*

1. Your company, its officers and management   1

2. Becoming a director 23

3. Your functions as a director 37

4. Your duties as a director to your company..................... 42

5. Your duties to your co-directors 51

6. Your responsibilities to your employees 60

7. Your accounting and financial responsibilities 72

8. Shareholders' meetings 80

9. Your remuneration as a director................................. 89

10. Your shareholding... 102

11. Ceasing to be a director... 108

12. Disqualification 115

13. Company investigations.. 124

14. Financial difficulties and company insolvency 128

Appendices.. 141

Bibliography 160

Index... 162

CONTENTS

INTRODUCTION

Unlike other recent books on directors' responsibilities, this book is designed to answer the questions actually asked by company directors (and some more that perhaps ought to be asked). Its question and answer format aims to make it easy to use.

Company law contains many provisions that affect anyone about to become a director for the first time. This book cannot attempt to cover all of these provisions comprehensively and we have not been able to cover the tax aspects of being a director in the pages available.

However, its content should enable a newly appointed director to grasp a basic knowledge of his responsibilities and will be a useful refresher to many acting directors of their responsibilities.

We hope that you will find this book a useful and straightforward guide to the responsibilities you will undertake as a director.

Stephen Copp and Alun Thomas.

ACKNOWLEDGEMENTS

The authors and publishers gratefully acknowledge with thanks the assistance given by Barry Johnson in editing the text and the kind permission of the following to reproduce material in this book:

The Institute of Directors for the extract on pages 19-21 from *Directors' Guide to Accounting and Auditing*.
Promotion of Non-Executive Directors (PRO NED) for Appendix II.

This book aims to provide general guidance only. Should the reader encounter particular problems he is advised to seek professional advice, which Deloitte Haskins & Sells would be pleased to provide.

While all reasonable care has been taken in the preparation of this book, no responsibility is accepted by the authors or Deloitte Haskins & Sells for any errors it may contain, or for any loss, howsoever occasioned, to any person by reliance on it.

References throughout the book to *he/him/himself* should be understood to refer also to *she/her/herself*.

1. YOUR COMPANY, ITS OFFICERS AND MANAGEMENT

Page

What is a company? 2

Why set up a company? 2

How is a company formed? 4

What is a company's Memorandum of Association? 5

What are a company's Articles of Association? 6

Should the Articles of Association make special provision for directors or will Table A do? 6

What are a company's 'statutory books'? 7

What is a company's 'registered office'? 8

What name can a company have? 8

Does a company have to trade under its registered name? 9

Can a company change its registered name? 9

What is a company seal? 10

What are the different types of company? 10

What legal provisions apply to companies? 12

Who owns a company? 14

Who runs a company? 14

Who are a company's 'officers'? 15

What is the significance of being a company officer? 15

Does a company need to have a company secretary? 15

Who can be a company secretary? 15

Does a company secretary also have to be a director? 16

What are the company secretary's responsibilities? 16

What happens when the company secretary is absent? Can a company appoint an assistant company secretary to take over? . 17

Does a company have to appoint an auditor? 17

How does a company appoint an auditor? 18

Who can be a company's auditor? 18

Can a company change its auditor? 19

What does an auditor do? 19

Does a company have to have a solicitor? 21

Who is the Registrar of Companies and what does it mean to 'file' documents with him? 21

What documents must be filed with the Registrar of Companies? 22

1. YOUR COMPANY, ITS OFFICERS AND MANAGEMENT

A company is a person, from a legal point of view albeit an artificial one. The *Companies Act 1985* says:

> From the date of incorporation mentioned in the certificate [of incorporation], the subscribers of the memorandum [of association], together with such other persons as may from time to time become members of the company, shall be a body corporate by the name contained in the memorandum [of association].

So, when you complete the formalities to set up a company, the company is recognised by the law as being a separate legal person from you. Although the law has developed an increasing number of exceptions to this rule, it still generally holds fast.

WHY SET UP A COMPANY?

Advantages

Limited liability
There can be little doubt that the majority of people who set up a company to carry on a business do so to obtain the advantage of limiting their liability for the debts and obligations of the business to the amount they contribute as capital on forming the company. However, there are a number of situations where the protection of limited liability can be lost, for example:

- Where a company's bankers or other creditors require a personal guarantee from its directors as a condition of giving the company finance, or of trading with it (see page 36).
- Where a director or shareholder is made liable to contribute to the assets of a company because of fraudulent or wrongful trading (see page 131).
- Where a director is involved in the management of a company in contravention of a disqualification order (see page 123).

In contrast, if you trade on your own account you are *always* personally liable for the debts and obligations you incur. Alternatively, if you carry on business in partnership with others you are *always* jointly liable with your other partners for the debts and obligations of the partnership. So there is, therefore, a real advantage in obtaining limited liability through incorporating your business as a company.

Commercial acceptability

If you incorporate a business you will frequently find that a company is more readily accepted by other businesses you wish to deal with. The reason for this is that the law governing companies is strict (for example, in relation to the audit requirement) and it is possible to find out far more about a company than about a sole trader or partnership.

Expansion

Because of the problems of personal liability, and the difficulties of obtaining finance, it is hard for a person trading on his own account to expand his business beyond a certain point. Even by entering into partnership with others these problems cannot wholly be overcome, because the *Companies Act 1985* prohibits the formation of trading partnerships that have twenty or more partners.

The company is an ideal vehicle for business expansion. Apart from there being no limit on the size of a company, the separation of ownership from management enables the owners of shares to sell their interest in the business in a relatively straightforward manner. Furthermore, a public company can market its shares to the public, provided that stringent conditions are fulfilled. This opens up the way to the Third Market, the Unlisted Securities Market and ultimately a full listing on The Stock Exchange, enabling the company to raise very large sums of finance.

Continuity

A company as a person will be legally unaffected by changes in its membership whether by death or transfer. Changes in a partnership will often bring about its dissolution and this can be administratively very inconvenient.

Taxation

Although the effects of taxation are not considered in this book there are occasions where carrying on business may be more advantageous via a company. This is a question on which professional advice should always be taken as the law is constantly changing.

Disadvantages

The main disadvantage you should consider before setting up a company is the burden of regulation upon those running it and the publicity that must be given to its affairs. This is in contrast to the almost total lack of regulation and the privacy enjoyed by sole traders and partnerships. Such regulation is not just an inconvenience, but can also be costly in financial terms. You should not necessarily let this discourage you, however, from carrying on a business through a company. Much of the legislation which places a burden upon you (for example, VAT and employment rules) applies equally to sole traders and partners.

Where you will be a director as well as a shareholder after setting up a company, you will take on major responsibilities. It is with these responsibilities that this book is concerned.

HOW IS A COMPANY FORMED?

The procedure which follows below is that used to form a private company limited by shares (the most common type of company formed). Other types of company may be formed and those are considered on page 10 below.

In practice, most companies are formed by specialised company formation agents and purchased 'off-the-shelf'. This method of formation is convenient and quick and your professional advisors should be able to assist you in the process. The cost of an off-the-shelf company will usually be in the region of £120.

Occasionally, there may be reasons why an off-the-shelf company is not suitable, for example, if you wish to include special provisions in the Memorandum or Articles of Association.

To form a company you need to send to the Registrar of Companies the following:

- The Memorandum of Association (see page 5 below).
- The Articles of Association (if Table A is not to be adopted) (see page 6 below).
- Form PUC 1 (The statement of capital on formation). This sets out the nominal share capital of the company and its subdivision into classes (if any). Capital duty must be paid when the shares are issued. The amount of this is calculated at 1% of the nominal value of the shares issued, or the consideration, whichever is greater. It is usual for the people who set up a company, 'the subscribers', to take only one share each. Where a company is formed off-the-shelf the subscribers will be employees of the solicitor or formation agent engaged to register the company, who later transfers the shares to the intended shareholders.
- Form 10 (The statement of first directors and secretary and intended situation of the registered office). This names the people who have agreed to act as the company's first directors and

secretary (together with their written consent) and gives the location of the company's registered office (see page 8).

- Form 12 (The declaration of compliance with the statutory requirements of the *Companies Act 1985*). This is a declaration that the requirements of the *Companies Act 1985* have been complied with. It is made either by the solicitor engaged in the formation of the company or by a director or the company secretary named.
- A fee, currently of £50.

Provided that these documents are in order, the Registrar of Companies will issue a Certificate of Incorporation. The company may then trade from the date given in the certificate.

WHAT IS A COMPANY'S MEMORANDUM OF ASSOCIATION?

The Memorandum of Association is a document which primarily sets out the purpose of a company. It must state:

- The company's name.
- Whether the registered office of the company is to be situated in England and Wales, or Scotland.
- The company's objects.
- That the liability of the company's members is limited.
- The amount of share capital that the company proposes to be registered with and its division into shares.

The most important clause is the one that sets out the company's objects. Companies are usually formed for some specific purpose or purposes. Company law intends these purposes to be crystallised in the objects clause. One of the more common reasons why a company is specially formed and not purchased off-the-shelf is because the objects clause needs to be individually drafted. The importance of the objects clause derives from the legal rule of *ultra vires*. This rule means that where a company acts outside the objects or powers given to it in its Memorandum of Association, that act is void. For various legal reasons this rule is of less importance nowadays, partly because objects clauses are so widely drafted that they give a company power to do almost anything that a natural person could do. Also, such wide objects clauses are included as a matter of course in the Memorandum of Association of companies purchased off-the-shelf.

WHAT ARE A COMPANY'S ARTICLES OF ASSOCIATION?

A company's Articles of Association are, in effect, its rule book, dealing with the detailed rules of the company's internal administration. On incorporation, a company may be registered with its own Articles of Association or, more commonly, it need not register any. In that situation 'Table A', which is a specimen set of Articles of Association, will be adopted as the company's own. Table A can be found in Statutory Instrument (SI) 1985 No 805, 'Companies (Tables A to F) Regulations 1985'. Frequently, companies will base their Articles of Association on Table A, but include their own modifications to it.

The current Table A deals with the following matters:

- The company's share capital.
- Company meetings.
- The number of directors.
- Alternate directors.
- The powers of directors.
- The delegation of directors' powers.
- The appointment and retirement of directors.
- The disqualification and removal of directors.
- The remuneration of directors.
- Directors' expenses.
- Directors' appointments and interests.
- Directors' gratuities and pensions.
- Directors' meetings.
- The company secretary.
- Minutes of meetings.
- The company seal.
- Dividends and the capitalisation of profits.
- Accounts.

You will appreciate from this that it is a good idea for you to familiarise yourself with the particular Articles of Association of a company before accepting appointment as a director of it.

SHOULD THE ARTICLES OF ASSOCIATION MAKE SPECIAL PROVISION FOR DIRECTORS OR WILL TABLE A DO?

Obviously, the answer to this question will depend on the particular circumstances of your company. Areas which commonly require consideration are:

- Whether, in the case of a private company, the company is to be permitted to have a sole director.
- Whether any maximum number of directors is to be specified.
- Whether the directors' right to exercise the company's power of borrowing should be limited in any way.
- Whether any special voting rights are to be conferred on any director(s).
- Whether a special *quorum* is desirable for board meetings (see page 52).
- Whether directors should have to retire by rotation and, if so, how (see page 110).
- Whether directors have the power to appoint an alternate director (see page 28).
- Whether the directors can appoint associate directors (see page 28), who are not directors for legal purposes.
- In the case of private companies, whether to give the directors power to refuse to register a transfer of shares.
- Whether the directors are to have the power to dismiss a director independently of the company in general meeting.

WHAT ARE A COMPANY'S STATUTORY BOOKS?

When you purchase a company off-the-shelf you will usually receive a number of impressive-looking bound books, referred to as the company's 'statutory books'. These have to be kept by law and made available for inspection by shareholders and members of the public. There are different rights of inspection, restrictions on the location of registers and permissible charges for inspection for each 'statutory book'. These are summarised in Appendix I.

The different 'statutory books' which must be kept are:

- The Register of Interests in Shares
  Public companies must maintain a register of their 'substantial shareholders', that is, holders of more than 5% who have notified their holdings in accordance with the law.
- The Register of Directors and Secretaries
  The obligation to maintain this is considered on page 22.
- The Register of Directors' Interests in Shares and Debentures
  The obligation to maintain this is considered on page 104.
- The Register of Members
  All companies must keep a register giving details of their shareholders.

- The Minute Book
  Minutes must be kept of shareholders', directors' and managers' meetings (see page 57).
- The Register of Charges
  All companies must keep a register giving details of charges over company property.
- The Register of Debenture Holders
  In fact, this is the only statutory book which a company is not obliged by law to keep. However, if a company does keep such a register it must be available for inspection.

In addition, directors' service contracts must be kept available for inspection (see page 34).

WHAT IS A COMPANY'S 'REGISTERED OFFICE'?

When a company is formed you need to give the location of the company's 'registered office' on Form 10. Furthermore, the company's Memorandum of Association must state whether the registered office of the company is to be situated in England and Wales, or Scotland.

The registered office of a company does not need to be the company's principal place of business, but may, for example, be its accountant's or solicitor's address, provided that the accountant or solicitor has agreed that the premises may be used as the registered office.

The main function of a company's registered office is to provide an official address for the company, in particular, for the service of legal documents. It is particularly important therefore where a company changes its location, that it notifies the Registrar of Companies (on Form No. 287 'Notice of change in situation of registered office') of the change of its registered office. The Registrar of Companies must be notified within fourteen days of the change. If this is not done, the company, its directors and its other officers, may be liable on summary conviction both to a £400 fine and, where the contravention continues, to a daily default fine of £40.

WHAT NAME CAN A COMPANY HAVE?

A company can be registered with any name subject to certain minimal restrictions:

- A company will not be registered with a name which duplicates or is too similar to the name of an existing company. However, the fact that the registration of a particular name is accepted is not conclusive of the company's right to be registered under that name. The DTI can order a company to change its name within twelve months of it being registered, if it considers that its name is the same as or too similar to that of an existing company name. Furthermore, if the effect of registering such a name is to pass one company's business off as being that of another company, the Courts may regard this as 'passing off'. In such a situation, the Court could grant an injunction to stop the use of the name as well as either an award of damages or an account of profits from using the name.

- A company will not be registered with a name which is offensive or which would constitute a criminal offence. Where a name is sensitive for some reason (for example, because it implies a connection with the government) the permission of the DTI is required. Furthermore, a company may be ordered to change its name if the DTI considers that it gives so misleading an indication of the company's business as to be likely to cause harm to the public.

- If the company is a private limited company its name *must* end with 'Limited' or 'Ltd.'. If it is a public company (see page 11) its name *must* end with 'public limited company' or 'p.l.c.'. These words must appear only at the *end* of the company's name. Where a company's sole objects are to promote commerce, art, science, education, religion, charity or a profession and its constitution requires its income to be applied for those objects and not distributed to members, the word 'limited' may be omitted.

DOES A COMPANY HAVE TO TRADE UNDER ITS REGISTERED NAME?

No. Frequently, for example, a company which is acquired off-the-shelf may have an unusual name. Rather than change the company's name it is common for the company to trade under a business name. If it does so, the company will be subject to the *Business Names Act 1985*. This prohibits the use of certain names and requires approval of others. It also requires disclosure of the company's registered name on business correspondence and at any business premises.

CAN A COMPANY CHANGE ITS REGISTERED NAME?

Yes. To do so the company's shareholders must pass a special resolution (see page 86), subject to similar considerations as to the choice of name on first registration (see above). It is usual upon a change of name for the company's Memorandum of Association to be altered and a footnote added to explain the change of name. Following the change of name the company will need to obtain a new Certificate of Incorporation from the Registrar of Companies.

WHAT IS A COMPANY SEAL?

As mentioned above, a company is an artificial person. The company seal can be regarded as that person's signature. When an off-the-shelf company is purchased, a seal, which is a metal stamp with the company's name engraved on it, will usually be acquired at the same time. It is usual for the company seal to be adopted and impressed in the company's minute book at the first directors' meeting.

The company seal is only required by law to be impressed upon a document which has to be under seal if it is executed by a natural person, that is a deed. When the seal is used in this way Table A requires that it is evidenced by the signatures of a director and either the company secretary (see page 16) or a second director. In practice, the company seal is impressed on a variety of documents (for example, commercial contracts) and the company secretary will record in a 'seal book' details of when it is used.

WHAT ARE THE DIFFERENT TYPES OF COMPANY?

Company law has given rise to a large number of classifications of companies depending, for example, on their size and purpose. There are four basic types of company:

- Private companies limited by shares
  These are by far the most common type of company. Unless otherwise stated, this book refers to such companies throughout. The distinguishing feature of these companies is that their names must end with the word 'Limited', although this can be abbreviated to 'Ltd.'.
- Private companies limited by guarantee without a share capital
  These companies are formed in basically the same way as other private companies and in general are subject to the same legal rules. They are usually formed for charitable, social or other non-trading purposes. Schools and colleges, professional and trade associations, clubs and management companies for blocks of flats are commonly established in this way.

The distinguishing features of such companies are:

- They may omit the word 'Limited' from their name, provided that they fulfil certain conditions, including an application to the Registrar of Companies.
- They have no share capital. Each member of the company instead has to undertake in the Memorandum of Association to contribute to the assets of the company if it is wound up. The extent of this guarantee is usually only £1.
- The Articles of Association, although based on Table A, are amended and can be found in SI 1985/805 Table C.

- Public companies limited by shares

  These companies are smaller in number and tend to be larger than private companies. Public company status is a precondition to a company applying for a Stock Exchange listing. Provided that certain conditions and procedures are followed, a private company may re-register as a public company.

  The distinguishing features of such companies are:

  - The Memorandum of Association must state that the company is to be a public company.
  - The name of the company must end with the words 'public limited company' which may be abbreviated to 'p.l.c.'. If the Memorandum of Association states that the company's registered office is to be in Wales, the name may alternatively end with the words 'cwmni cyfyngedig cyhoeddus', which may be abbreviated to 'c.c.c.'.
  - A public company may, provided that it satisfies various conditions, offer its shares to the public.
  - A public company, once it has been incorporated, must not do business or borrow unless the Registrar of Companies has issued it with a certificate. This certificate cannot be obtained unless a director or the secretary of the company has filed a statutory declaration on Form 117 with the Registrar of Companies. This declaration must state that the nominal value of the company's allotted share capital is no less than £50,000. Because only a quarter of this needs to be paid up, a public company can in fact be set up with a paid up capital of only £12,500.

There are a variety of legal rules applicable to public companies which do not apply to private companies. However, these differences are outside the scope of this book.

- Unlimited companies
  As the name suggests, an unlimited company is one where the members may be required to contribute *all* their assets to the company in a winding up to the extent that the company cannot pay its debts. As mentioned on page 2, the protection of limited liability can be illusory in certain circumstances. In these circumstances, there can be some advantage to setting up an unlimited company (for example, an unlimited company may not need to file its accounts with the Registrar of Companies). As a result, the accounts of unlimited companies are not open for public inspection. Hence, financial institutions are occasionally established in this way.

WHAT LEGAL PROVISIONS APPLY TO COMPANIES?

If this book were a thousand pages long it still might not be possible to answer this question fully! The law applicable to companies derives from a number of sources – statute, the decisions of the Courts and, increasingly, directly effective provisions of European Community law. On top of this, there is a mass of non-legal regulation that companies may have to follow, for example, Statements of Standard Accounting Practice and, in the case of listed companies, The Stock Exchange's Yellow Book. The main categories of legislation that you will need to consider are as follows:

Company law
The principal pieces of legislation you need to be aware of are:

- The *Companies Act 1985*
  This Act is the main codification of company law. It deals with:

  - The formation of companies.
  - Company names.
  - Company powers.
  - The increase, maintenance and reduction of a company's share capital.
  - Accounting and auditing requirements.
  - Company management – the qualifications, duties and responsibilities of directors and secretaries.
  - The enforcement of fair dealing by directors.
  - Company investigations.
  - The protection of a company's members against unfair prejudice.
  - Overseas companies.

- The *Company Directors Disqualification Act 1986*
  This Act is dealt with in Chapter 12 below. As you will appreciate from its title, its purpose is self-explanatory.
- The *Insolvency Act 1986*
  This Act deals with:

  - Company voluntary arrangements.
  - Administration orders.
  - Receivership.
  - Winding up of companies.

- The *Company Securities (Insider Dealing) Act 1985*
  The purpose of this Act is, again, self-explanatory, as is its recent popularity as reading material in the City of London. Its implications are dealt with in Chapter 10.
- The *Prevention of Fraud (Investments) Act 1958*
  Although the repeal of this Act is imminent, with the enactment of the *Financial Services Act 1986,* it is still important because it lays down penalties for fraudulently inducing people to invest money.
- The *Financial Services Act 1986*
  Under this Act various organisations have been set up to regulate and control companies and other entities that undertake investment business.
- The *Theft Act 1968*
  Although the title of this Act may not make it seem immediately relevant, it deals with:

  - Certain offences of fraud.
  - The liability of company officers for offences by the company.
  - False statements by company directors.

Tax law

All companies and their directors are well advised to seek professional advice on how tax law affects both them and their companies.

Employment law

A brief overview of your obligations in law to your employees is given in Chapter 6.

Other

As you will appreciate there are hundreds of other obligations the law lays upon companies and their directors which cannot be described in detail in this book. Examples are the consumer protection legislation, the law of landlord and tenant and environmental law. The Institute of Directors has published a valuable book on this subject called *Directors' Personal Liabilities* (1984), which is a useful starting point. In addition, some specialised businesses are subject to additional regulation. For example, insurance companies are regulated by the *Insurance Companies Act 1982*. This book only considers the position of ordinary companies.

WHO OWNS A COMPANY?

A company is owned by its shareholders. However, you must not confuse this type of ownership with the ownership of the company's assets. Because a company is a separate legal entity, the company itself owns its assets. As a shareholder, you do not even have an insurable interest in the assets of your company – they belong to it and not you.

WHO RUNS A COMPANY?

Lord Denning summarised the responsibility for managing a company in this way:

> A company may in many ways be likened to a human body. It has a brain and nerve centre which controls what it does. It also has hands which hold the tools and act in accordance with directions from the centre. Some of the people in the company are mere servants and agents who are nothing more than hands to do the work and cannot be said to represent the mind or will. Others are directors and managers who represent the directing mind and will of the company and control what it does. The state of mind of these managers is the state of mind of the company and is treated by the law as such. So you will find in cases where the law requires personal fault as a condition of liability in tort, the fault of the manager will be the personal fault of the company. . . . . So also in the criminal law, in cases where the law requires a guilty mind as a condition of a criminal offence, the guilty mind of the directors or the managers will render the company itself guilty. . . . . Whether their intention is the company's intention depends on the nature of the matter under consideration, the relative position of the officer or agent, and the other relevant facts and circumstances of the case.

The important question then is 'who are a company's officers?'

WHO ARE A COMPANY'S 'OFFICERS'?

The *Companies Act 1985* defines the officers of a company as including the directors, managers and the company secretary. The Courts have also taken the view that the company's auditor should usually be regarded as an officer. A company's bankers and solicitors will not usually be officers unless they have other duties and, consequently, occupy a position in the company different from that of a normal banker or solicitor.

WHAT IS THE SIGNIFICANCE OF BEING A COMPANY OFFICER?

The officers of a company are those who are regarded by the law as being accountable for it. For example, many of the criminal offences contained in the *Companies Act 1985* may be committed by any officer of the company, although some apply only to directors (see Appendix III). Furthermore, the financial statements of a company must disclose various transactions with a company's officers (see page 99).

DOES A COMPANY NEED TO HAVE A COMPANY SECRETARY?

Yes. This is a legal requirement for every company. However, you can obtain company secretarial services from most firms of chartered accountants or solicitors.

WHO CAN BE A COMPANY SECRETARY?

Anyone can be the company secretary of a private company. In a typical small company it will be usual for there to be two directors, one of whom is also appointed company secretary.

In the case of a public company, the directors must take all reasonable steps to secure that the secretary of the company has the requisite knowledge and experience to discharge the functions of company secretary. Furthermore, to be eligible to be company secretary of a public company, a person must satisfy one of the following conditions. He must:

- Have been company secretary, or assistant or deputy company secretary on 22 December 1980 to the company in question.
- Have been the company secretary of a public company for at least three of the five years immediately preceding his appointment.
- Be a member of either:

- The Institute of Chartered Accountants in England and Wales.
- The Institute of Chartered Accountants of Scotland.
- The Chartered Association of Certified Accountants.
- The Institute of Chartered Accountants in Ireland.
- The Institute of Chartered Secretaries and Administrators.
- The Chartered Institute of Management Accountants.
- The Chartered Institute of Public Finance and Accountancy.

- Be a barrister, advocate or solicitor called or admitted in any part of the UK.
- Be a person who, either because he holds or has held any other position or because he is a member of any other body, appears to the directors to be capable of discharging the functions of a company secretary.

DOES A COMPANY SECRETARY ALSO HAVE TO BE A DIRECTOR?

No. Although this is usual in small private companies it is not a legal requirement.

WHAT ARE THE COMPANY SECRETARY'S RESPONSIBILITIES?

As noted on page 15, a company secretary is an officer of the company. He may also be a director and/or an employee of the company. The role of the company secretary has become increasingly important as the legal regulation of companies has developed. For example, some company secretaries will become responsible for the compliance function within their company, made necessary by the *Financial Services Act 1986*. Traditionally, the company secretary has been responsible for company administration. His duties include the convening of board and company meetings on the direction of the board, taking minutes of meetings, writing up the company's statutory books, and filing returns with the Registrar of Companies. Unless the company uses external share registrars, the company secretary will also deal with share transfers. Because of the legal nature of the role, frequently a company secretary will be a solicitor or barrister, who will be involved in other aspects of the company's legal work (for example, negotiating and drafting contracts, ensuring patents and copyrights are protected and dealing with employment law questions). As Lord Denning put it, the company secretary:

"Is an officer of the company with extensive duties and responsibilities . . . He is no longer a mere clerk. He regularly makes representations on behalf of the company and enters into contracts on its behalf which come within the day to day running of the company's business, so much so that he may be regarded as held out as having authority to do such things on behalf of the company. He is certainly entitled to sign contracts connected with the administrative side of a company's affairs, such as employing staff, and ordering cars, and so forth. All such matters, now come within the ostensible authority of a company secretary."

WHAT HAPPENS WHEN THE COMPANY SECRETARY IS ABSENT? CAN A COMPANY APPOINT AN ASSISTANT COMPANY SECRETARY TO TAKE OVER?

Only the company secretary can validly perform the duties of the company secretary. The *Companies Act 1985* permits an assistant or deputy company secretary to do so, but only where there is no company secretary or none capable of acting. To avoid the difficulties that this may cause, the *Companies Act 1985* permits a company to appoint more than one person as company secretary, who then act as joint secretaries. However, this would generally only be necessary and practicable where the duties of the company secretary are particularly onerous.

DOES A COMPANY HAVE TO APPOINT AN AUDITOR?

Yes. When a company is incorporated an auditor must be appointed, either by the directors, or if they fail to do so, by the shareholders. This auditor holds office only until the end of the first general meeting at which the company's accounts are presented, and he may then be re-appointed.

An existing company must appoint an auditor at each general meeting it holds where its annual accounts are presented. This normally happens at the company's annual general meeting. The auditor will then hold office until the next such meeting. If, for any reason, the company ceases to have an auditor between meetings, the directors, (or if they fail to do so, the shareholders) may appoint a new auditor.

If for any reason a company has no auditor, the Secretary of State for Trade and Industry must be notified within a week, and he may then appoint an auditor himself.

HOW DOES A COMPANY APPOINT AN AUDITOR?

An ordinary resolution of the company's shareholders is all that is needed to re-appoint an existing auditor or its first auditor, although special notice is required to re-appoint a company's first auditor. The auditor should send you an 'engagement letter' which is intended to clearly define the extent of the auditor's responsibilities and, therefore, to minimise the risk of any misunderstanding in the work that he may carry out. It is useful for a company's directors to discuss the contents of the engagement letter with the proposed auditor *prior* to his appointment, because the letter of engagement will form the basis of the contract between the company and the auditor. Accordingly, you should confirm your agreement to the engagement letter in writing. The matters it will usually contain are:

- The responsibilities of the directors and the auditor respectively in relation to the audit and any irregularities or fraud.
- The nature and scope of any other service to be supplied by the auditor, for example, accounting, taxation or consultancy services.
- The basis on which fees are to be computed, rendered and paid.

WHO CAN BE A COMPANY'S AUDITOR?

Usually, only a member of one of the following bodies may be appointed:

- The Institute of Chartered Accountants in England and Wales.
- The Institute of Chartered Accountants of Scotland.
- The Institute of Chartered Accountants in Ireland.
- The Chartered Association of Certified Accountants.

Under special circumstances, usually involving DTI approval, a person who is not a member of one of these bodies may be an auditor, but this is very rare.

More importantly, certain persons who are connected in some way with a company are prohibited by law from being the company's auditor. These include:

- A director of the company.
- The company secretary.
- An employee of the company.
- A corporate body.

In all these situations a partner or employee of the person is also prohibited from being the company's auditor or from acting as auditor of any group company.

Any person who acts as an auditor knowing that he is disqualified from appointment commits a criminal offence.

CAN A COMPANY CHANGE ITS AUDITOR?

Yes, but for obvious reasons, the law makes this difficult to do.

Special notice (see page 83) is required for a resolution at a general meeting of a company to remove an auditor or to appoint an auditor other than the retiring auditor. This also applies if the resolution is to fill a casual vacancy in the office of auditor or to reappoint a retiring auditor who was appointed in that way.

A copy of this resolution has to be sent to the proposed auditor and also to the retiring or resigning auditor who is not proposed for reappointment. The retiring auditor not proposed for reappointment is entitled to make written representations to the company and require the company to circulate these to shareholders. If this is not done, the auditor may require them to be read out at general meeting.

You will also find that the new auditor is required, as a matter of professional etiquette, to write to the outgoing auditor to ask whether there is any reason why he should not accept the appointment. This also provides a sanction against companies who might wish to change their auditor for other than good reasons.

If a company does adopt a resolution to remove an auditor before his term of office expires, the company must give notice on Form 386 to the Registrar of Companies within fourteen days.

WHAT DOES AN AUDITOR DO?

This was summed up by Matthew Patient, Chairman of the Auditing Practices Committee, in an article 'Auditing - an Explanation' in the *Director's Guide to 'Accounting and Auditing'* (Institute of Directors, 1986) in the following way:

The *Companies Act 1985* requires auditors to report to shareholders whether the financial statements (and these include both company and group financial statements) have been properly prepared in accordance with the Act and whether or not in their opinion those give a true and fair view. The auditor is also obliged to state by exception in his audit report if proper accounting records have not been kept, or if the information in the Directors' Report is not consistent with the accounts and other similar matters. He has to disclose certain information such as loans to directors and directors' remuneration if the accounts do not do so. Note that the obligation to prepare accounts remains with the directors. The auditor has only to report on the financial statements, not be responsible for preparing them. Also the term 'true and fair' is not defined in law. There is almost certainly more than one 'true and fair' view in most instances and the auditor is giving an opinion on whether or not the director's approach taken in the accounts is a 'true and fair' view.

In support of the legal obligations imposed on auditors there are professional standards and guidelines issued by the Auditing Practices Committee and other accountancy profession authorities. These describe matters to which auditors should have regard in performing their work to a satisfactory quality. Neither in law nor under their professional guidelines are auditors responsible for the prevention or detection of irregularities or fraud. This remains with management . . .

The auditor . . . has rights to attend and be heard at general meetings, rights of access to the company and rights to require information and explanations from the company's officers. There are sanctions on directors and other officers who make false statements to auditors which are 'misleading, false and deceptive in a material particular' . . .

At the outset the auditor will agree the terms of his engagement with his client [see page 18]. He will then plan how to perform the audit efficiently. Initially he will obtain information about the business, its areas of risk and the accounting policies the company adopts. Appropriate staff will be allocated and visits timed hopefully to fit in with the client's timetable.

The auditor obtains the assurance he requires by testing transactions (he cannot check everything as this will be too expensive and time consuming) after taking into account the materiality of the information being processed and the reliability of the system. This requires him to ascertain the reasonableness of the client's own system of accounting and to test it qualitatively. He will also concentrate on high risk areas and significant or unusual transactions.

He will need to obtain audit evidence by observing the way in which the operations are carried out and inspecting independent evidence such as invoices and statements. He will seek independent confirmation and representations from third parties where appropriate – these will include debtors, creditors and banks. He will review the financial statements concentrating on such matters as valuation of stocks, provisions for doubtful debts and disclosure of contingent liabilities. At the end of his work he will discuss any problems with [you], hopefully agree whatever amendments are necessary, and finally sign an unqualified audit report . . .

Beside the legalistic, but nonetheless important, aspect of having a second opinion on the financial statements, management can obtain other benefits from the audit. The auditor usually has considerable experience and expertise. He can usefully comment on [*your*] affairs from the information obtained during the course of the audit. Such comments might extend to the quality of staff, the effectiveness of an accounting department, or the accuracy of the management information system.

DOES A COMPANY HAVE TO HAVE A SOLICITOR?

There is no legal requirement for a company to appoint a solicitor, as there is for it to appoint an auditor. In fact, there is no specific office as such that a solicitor could be appointed to, although clearly a solicitor can be appointed to general offices, such as director or company secretary. However, it is probably best practice for a company to deal with most of its legal business through one firm of solicitors, so that they have an opportunity to gain an understanding of the company's business and needs.

WHO IS THE REGISTRAR OF COMPANIES AND WHAT DOES IT MEAN TO 'FILE' DOCUMENTS WITH HIM?

At various places in this book you will come across references to 'filing' documents with the 'Registrar of Companies'. The Registrar of Companies for England and Wales is responsible for the Companies Registration Office in England and Wales. There is a separate Registrar and Companies Registration Office in Scotland.

● The address of the Registrar of Companies for England and Wales is:

Companies Registration Office,
Crown Way,
Maindy,
CARDIFF CF4 3UZ.

- The address of the Registrar of Companies for Scotland is:

Exchequer Chambers,
102 George Street,
EDINBURGH EH2 3DJ.

- Additional facilities (for inspecting company records) are maintained at:

Companies' House,
55-71 City Road,
LONDON EC1Y 1BB.

To file a document, it is simply necessary to send it addressed to the Registrar of Companies at the appropriate Companies Registration Office.

WHAT DOCUMENTS MUST BE FILED
WITH THE REGISTRAR OF COMPANIES?

There are a vast number of documents which may have to be filed with the Registrar of Companies, depending upon your company's circumstances. The principal ones which you are likely to need to consider are:

- The company formation documents (see page 4).
- The notice of change of directors or secretaries or in their particulars (Form 288). This will need to be filed, for example, if a director changes his address.
- The annual return of a company (Form 363).
- Particulars of a mortgage or charge (Form 395).
- The forms relating to changing from private to public company status (Forms 43(3), 43(3)(e) and 117).
- The notice of a company's first accounting reference date or a new accounting reference date (Forms 224, 225(1) and 225(2)). Remember, the first of these must be filed within six months of the incorporation of a company.

2. BECOMING A DIRECTOR

	Page
Am I eligible to be a director?	24
What should I find out about a company before accepting appointment?	24
Can I hold more than one directorship?	27
I already do the same job as the other directors and attend board meetings. Am I in fact a director?	27
I've been promoted to 'Director of Marketing'. I am a real director, aren't I?	28
I've been asked to be an 'alternate director'. What does that mean?	28
What are the formalities attached to being appointed an alternate director?	29
I've been asked to be a 'nominee director'. What does that mean?	29
I've heard of 'shadow directors'. What are they?	30
What are the implications of being a shadow director?	30
I've been asked to be a 'non-executive director' of a company. What does this entail?	31
Are there any formalities on being appointed a director?	32
If I become a director of a company will I be one of its employees?	33
Should I have a service contract with my company?	33
What terms should be included in my service contract?	34
Will the shareholders be able to see any of the terms of my service contract?	34
Will the shareholders have to approve any of the terms of my service contract?	35
Will my name appear on the company notepaper?	35
I've been asked by the company's bankers to give a guarantee of its bank overdraft. Should I?	36

2. BECOMING A DIRECTOR

AM I ELIGIBLE TO BE A DIRECTOR?

Almost anybody can be a company director. The law does not require any qualifications before a person can be made a director, although certain categories of person may not be. However, surprisingly, a minor, an alien or a mentally ill person *may* be a director. Furthermore, as any legal person can be a director, so can a company. There are the following exceptions to these general rules:

- Where the Articles of Association of a company impose any special requirements for qualification or disqualification. For example, under the current Table A you will cease to be a director if:
  - You are prohibited by law and, in particular, the *Companies Act 1985* from being a director.
  - You become bankrupt or make any arrangements or composition with your creditors.
  - You satisfy certain conditions relating to mental disorder.
  - You resign by notice.
  - You are absent from board meetings without the other directors' permission for more than six consecutive months and they resolve that your office be vacated.
- Where you have been disqualified from being a director by the Courts (see Chapter 12).
- You may not be made a director of a *public* company or a *subsidiary* of a *public* company if you are seventy years old or more, unless your appointment is made or approved by the shareholders in general meeting when you reach the age of seventy. Further, if you are aware that you are being proposed for appointment or reappointment (say, by rotation) and you are over this age limit, you must give notice of this to the company.

WHAT SHOULD I FIND OUT ABOUT A COMPANY BEFORE ACCEPTING APPOINTMENT?

Clearly, your approach to accepting appointment as a director will depend on whether or not you are a stranger to the company. If you are already a senior manager of a company, you may have extensive knowledge of your company's affairs, although possibly only in respect of a limited part of it. If you are to be appointed from outside, or are asked to be a non-executive director of a company, you may have little or no knowledge of it. In either case, you are well advised to find out as much as you can about your company, in the light of the responsibilities you are to take on.

Basic sources of information include those noted below. Generally, these sources can be used to investigate 'standing' information (for example, addresses, trade names, markets served, number of employees, bankers and similar information) for a company or a group.

COMPANIES' HOUSE
All information required to be filed by law can be obtained personally, or by using one of the many agencies specialising in obtaining such information.

DIRECTORY OF DIRECTORS
An annual publication listing directors of major companies and identifying all directorships held by them.

DUN & BRADSTREET
A major credit reference agency that will provide credit ratings as well as detailed information of use in assessing companies, including newspaper reports. The information is also maintained on a computer database.

EXTEL CARDS
A card index that provides detailed financial information primarily about listed companies and certain general information.

KEY BRITISH ENTERPRISES
A four volume book that provides financial and basic information on the nature and size of companies' businesses, including products and services. It is also useful for identifying companies in similar businesses.

KOMPASS
A two volume book that provides basic information on the nature and size of companies' businesses, including details of their products and services. It is also useful for identifying companies in similar businesses.

MACMILLAN'S UNQUOTED COMPANIES
A book providing summary financial information on leading UK unquoted companies.

STOCK EXCHANGE OFFICIAL YEARBOOK
A book containing a broad range of information relating to The Stock Exchange, and also to those people and companies who are involved with it.

TEXTLINE
A computer database giving up to date information on companies from press releases, news reports, etc.

WHO OWNS WHOM
A two volume book that is designed to help anyone wishing to identify relationships between companies.

The following sources will assist you to make comparisons between the results of a company and other companies in the same industrial sector or between a company and the industrial sector average.

DATASTREAM
An on-line database that maintains extensive information on a wide variety of matters of financial, business and economic interest.

INTER-COMPANY-COMPARISONS
An on-line database designed to provide information on, and facilitate comparisons between, over 60,000 UK companies.

In addition, useful information can be obtained from the financial press.

The areas which you should particularly address are:

- Whether the company is a going concern.
  This may be difficult to ascertain unless you have access to internal information. The most obvious place to look will be to see whether the accounts are prepared on a going concern basis or the audit report qualified. Otherwise, the basic consideration will be whether the company appears able to meet its debts as they fall due. Indications to the contrary will often include:

  - Recurring operating losses.
  - Heavy dependence on short-term finance for long-term needs.
  - Working capital deficiencies.
  - Low liquidity ratios.
  - High or increasing debt to equity gearing ratios.
  - Undercapitalisation, in particular, a deficiency on share capital and reserves.

- Inter-group guarantees indicating a dependence on a holding company.
- Major contingent liabilities, for example, litigation over the right to produce the company's product.

   None of these are ever conclusive, however, and you should look carefully at the positive aspects of a company as well; for example, the value of its assets and strength of its management.

- The integrity of the company's management.
- The company's position compared with its competitors.
- The detailed terms to be included in your service contract.

CAN I HOLD MORE THAN ONE DIRECTORSHIP?

Yes. As an individual, you may hold any number of directorships you wish. Particulars of these other directorships must be included on Form 288 (Notice of change of directors or secretaries or in their particulars – see page 22 above) and filed with the Registrar of Companies.

It is likely where a large number of directorships are held that some of these directorships will be non-executive (see page 31) and, therefore, that there may be no legal requirement for continuous attention to be given to the affairs of one company. However, if you are contemplating accepting appointment to a number of directorships, you should consider fully whether you have the time to deal with the affairs of each company. Otherwise, there is a risk that you will, through inadvertence, face disqualification (see Chapter 12).

Furthermore, the more directorships you hold, the more likely you are to find yourself placed in a conflict of interest between competing companies. You are not prevented from being the director of a rival company. However, the Courts are willing to restrain a director of one company, by injunction, from disclosing trade secrets or confidential information about one company to a rival company of which he is also a director.

I ALREADY DO THE SAME JOB AS THE OTHER DIRECTORS AND ATTEND BOARD MEETINGS. AM I IN FACT A DIRECTOR?

You may well be. Company law defines a director as 'any person occupying the position of a director, by whatever name called'. The reason for this is that some companies (for example schools which operate as a company) prefer not to use the title 'director', but are managed in fact by a board of 'governors' or a 'management committee'. Where such individuals have the same function as a 'director', the law regards them as such. In your situation, you are unlikely to be regarded as a director unless, in addition, you actively take part in board meetings and vote at them. If you think you may be a director, however, you really ought to seek professional advice as you may risk being regarded as one.

I'VE BEEN PROMOTED TO 'DIRECTOR OF MARKETING'. I AM A REAL DIRECTOR, AREN'T I?

As in the situation above, the answer to this question will depend on whether you occupy the position, of a director, and not on your title. The risk is that if you do not sit on the board, you will not have access to the information you need to ascertain what the company's position really is. Yet you may still be treated as a director for legal purposes. It is a fine distinction, but the Institute of Directors (*Guidelines for Directors* 1985/6) says that "'Director of . . .' is generally accepted as implying that the holder of the title does not sit on the board, while ' . . . Director' is usually taken to imply that he does." However, the fact that your title contains the word 'director' must strongly imply that you *are* a director.

The same considerations apply to anyone who is given what is termed an 'associate' directorship, which includes being called a 'regional', 'area' or 'divisional' director.

I'VE BEEN ASKED TO BE AN 'ALTERNATE DIRECTOR'. WHAT DOES THAT MEAN?

What it means to be an 'alternate director' will depend upon the Articles of Association of your company. If these are based on Table A your position will be as follows. Any director of your company has the power to appoint a person to be an alternate director and to remove that person. If the person that he wishes to appoint is not already a director (as will usually be the case) then the board must approve the appointment by resolution. Your appointment as an alternate director is dependent upon the person who appointed you remaining a director. If he ceases to be a director for any reason, you will cease to be an alternate director automatically. The only exception to this is where the director who appointed you ceases to be a director and is deemed re-appointed (for example, where the Articles of Association provide for retirement by rotation (see page 110)).

28

As an alternate director, you are regarded by the law as a full director of your company. Although the relationship between you and the director who appoints you may bear some similarities to that of principal and agent, this is not how the law regards it. In the absence of the director who appointed you, you will be entitled to do all that he can do. Therefore, you will, in the usual way, be entitled to notice of board meetings and notice of committee meetings where the appointing director is a member. However, you are only entitled to attend and to vote at board meetings when the director who appointed you is *absent*.

WHAT ARE THE FORMALITIES ATTACHED TO BEING APPOINTED AN ALTERNATE DIRECTOR?

As noted above, company law regards an alternate director as a full director. Consequently, the appointment of an alternate director should be notified to the Registrar of Companies as a change of director on Form 288 (Notice of change of directors or secretaries or in their particulars). You would also have to be disclosed as a director in the company's annual accounts.

Table A requires the appointment or removal of an alternate director to be notified to the company in writing signed by the director (or in some other manner approved by the directors).

I'VE BEEN ASKED TO BE A 'NOMINEE DIRECTOR'. WHAT DOES THAT MEAN?

A 'nominee director' is usually understood to mean a director who is appointed to the board of a company on the 'nomination', that is, the request, of a party outside of that company. Common situations where such an appointment is made are:

- Where a joint venture company is set up by two companies and the Articles of Association of the joint venture company or other agreement provide for the appointment of such directors.
- Where an investor in a company wishes to maintain some control over his investment.

The formalities for such an appointment are the same as those for the other categories of director discussed above. Equally the powers and the responsibilities of a nominee director are the same as for other directors. This is particularly important to bear in mind if you are offered such an appointment. A director's duties are owed to his company. As discussed above, there is no prohibition on a director holding directorships of more than one company, *provided only* that this does not lead to any conflict of interest. Where it does, as a nominee directorship frequently could, the individual director concerned would be at risk of being liable to the company that he was a nominee director of for any damage done. The full ramifications of this are considered in the Institute of Directors' booklet *Guide to Boardroom Practice – Nominee Directors* (1985). It would make little difference in this context whether or not the director appointed as nominee was, in fact, a director of the nominating company or not, if such a conflict of interest could be shown.

Companies considering the appointment of a nominee to another company should also take into account the possibility of being regarded as a 'shadow director' of that company and the effect that that might have upon them (see below).

I'VE HEARD OF 'SHADOW DIRECTORS'. WHAT ARE THEY?

You can be a shadow director of a company without being formally appointed a director of it. All that the law requires is that the directors of a company are accustomed to act in accordance with your directions or instructions. The only exception to this rule is where the directors act on advice given by you in your professional capacity alone (for example, if you are the company's accountant). Therefore if, for example, you own some shares in a company and the directors invariably do what you say, you will be a shadow director.

WHAT ARE THE IMPLICATIONS OF BEING A SHADOW DIRECTOR?

Various provisions of the *Companies Act 1985* relating to directors will apply to you. These provisions, in the order in which they appear in the *Companies Act 1985*, relate to:

- The register of directors and secretaries.
- The inclusion of directors' names on business correspondence.
- The duty of directors to have regard to the interests of employees as well as members.
- The disclosure of directors' interests in contracts and transactions with the company.
- Publicity in respect of directors' service contracts.

- The need for the duration of the directors' contracts of employment to be approved by a general meeting.
- The need for the terms of contracts for the acquisition of substantial amounts of assets by or from directors to be approved by a general meeting.
- The prohibition on directors buying options to purchase or sell shares or debentures issued by the company or companies to the same group.
- The duty of directors to report the acquisition or disposal of an interest in shares and debentures of the company or of other companies in the same group.
- The restrictions imposed on loans, quasi-loans and credit transactions for the benefit of directors and their connected persons and their disclosure in the company's financial statements.
- The reporting of transactions such as those mentioned directly above in the company's annual accounts.
- The annual return of the company.

In addition, various provisions of the *Insolvency Act 1986* are applied to shadow directors, in particular those relating to wrongful trading (see Chapter 12). Also, some of the provisions of the *Company Directors Disqualification Act 1986* are applied to shadow directors, in particular, the duty of the Court to disqualify unfit directors of insolvent companies (see also Chapter 12).

I'VE BEEN ASKED TO BE A NON-EXECUTIVE DIRECTOR OF A COMPANY. WHAT DOES THIS ENTAIL?

An executive director is usually an employee of a company and has an executive function within it. A non-executive director will not be an employee of the company and will frequently be appointed on a part-time basis only.

Your legal powers and duties will be the same if you become a non-executive director as if you were an executive director. Because of this, you should ensure that you will have the same access to information within the company as other directors have. However, your duties as a director will be intermittent and you are not, therefore, required to give continuous attention to your company's affairs.

PRO NED, an organisation established to promote non-executive directors, summarises the purpose of non-executive directors in the *Role of the Non-Executive Director* (1982) as being 'to provide the board with knowledge, expertise, judgement and balance, which may not be available if the Board consists only of full-time executives'. In the context of the board, this can involve:

- Seeing issues in their totality.
- Giving the external view.
- Providing special skills.
- Providing an independent view where potential conflicts of interest arise.
- Providing contacts, for example, with sources of finance.
- Advising on the public presentation of the company's activities and performance.

Outside the context of the board, this can include:
- Advising the chairman generally and, in particular, on succession to top management positions.
- Advising on board and top management structure.
- Advising on the adequacy of financial and other information available.
- Advising on the structure and level of remuneration of executive directors.
- Acting as a member of a committee set up by the board to study a particular subject or area of operations.

A *Code of Recommended Practice on Non-Executive Directors* issued by PRO NED is included in Appendix II of this book.

If your company is listed on The Stock Exchange its financial statements must include a statement of the identity of the independent non-executive directors together with a short biographical note on each. The note in the Yellow Book to this requirement also refers to the PRO NED *Code of Recommended Practice* and says that the Quotations Committee 'support the policy of PRO NED and the implementation of this Code'.

ARE THERE ANY FORMALITIES ON BEING APPOINTED A DIRECTOR?

Yes. If you are to be a director when a company is first formed, you will need to be named on Form 10 (Situation of Registered Office). This should give details of your full name and address, business occupation, nationality, date of birth, and any other directorships you may hold. You must sign the form to indicate that you consent to act as a director of the company. The form must be sent to the Registrar of Companies at the same time as the proposed company's Memorandum of Association.

If you are being appointed a director of an existing company, a Form 288 (Nature of Change of Directors or Secretaries or in their Particulars) will need to be completed. The information required is the same as that required on Form 10 above, but must additionally state the date of appointment. Form 288 must be sent to the Registrar of Companies within fourteen days of the change.

If the company is listed on The Stock Exchange, the appointment must be notified immediately to The Stock Exchange. A new director may be required to submit a detailed declaration as well. Furthermore, any important change in the holding of an executive office must be notified to The Stock Exchange Company Announcement Office.

In addition, the appointment of a director must always be recorded in the company's own Register of Directors and Secretaries. The details to be recorded are the same as required on Forms 10 and 288. Any changes in the particulars (including any change of address) must also be notified within fourteen days to the Registrar of Companies on Form 288.

IF I BECOME A DIRECTOR OF A COMPANY WILL I BE ONE OF ITS EMPLOYEES?

This will depend upon the nature of your appointment. If you are an executive director you will invariably be an employee as well. However, if you are a non-executive director then you may not be an employee. In that case, you are what is known in legal terms as an 'office holder' (not to be confused with the 'office holder' referred to in the context of a company's insolvency). One example of the effects of the distinction is that you will receive a salary as an employee, but fees as an office holder.

SHOULD I HAVE A SERVICE CONTRACT WITH MY COMPANY?

If you are an executive director then you will be an employee of the company. Your terms of employment will be contained in your service contract with the company. Basic particulars of your terms of employment must be given to you in a written statement so as to satisfy the *Employment Protection (Consolidation) Act 1978*, which is the situation with all employees. As an executive director, however, it is usual for you to have a full written service contract with your company which deals with your rights and responsibilities to your company and *vice-versa*.

WHAT TERMS SHOULD BE INCLUDED IN MY SERVICE CONTRACT?

The terms of your service contract will depend on your particular circumstances and those of your company. Consequently, it is never wise to make use of any 'model' service contract without taking professional advice on whether it needs to be amended. However, you should not be surprised to see terms with the following effect:

- That your duties and powers will be those that the board will subsequently delegate to you.
- That you must comply with any decision of the board.
- That you must devote the whole of your time and attention to your company's business. This may be combined with a provision that you will not undertake any other occupation whilst being a director of the company.
- That you will treat as confidential any information that you obtain because of your position within the company both whilst a director and thereafter.
- That you will not compete with the company if you cease to be a director of it. To be valid this will usually be limited to a period of time and geographical area.

In addition, the service contract will contain clauses dealing with:

- Your remuneration and benefits.
- Any compensation you are entitled to for loss of office.
- How your service contract may be terminated.
- The period of duration of your service contract. (Note, this may need approval by the company's shareholders. This is discussed on page 35.)

WILL THE SHAREHOLDERS BE ABLE TO SEE ANY OF THE TERMS OF MY SERVICE CONTRACT?

Yes. All companies must keep a copy of your service contract with the company and its subsidiaries at the company's registered office, principal place of business, or where it maintains its Register of Members. If there is no written service contract, a written memorandum of the terms on which you serve must be kept. In either situation, all changes in the terms of the contract made since it was entered into must be shown. However, your company need not keep any copy or memorandum of your contract if it has less than a year to run or can be terminated within a year without compensation.

Your company does not have to keep a copy of your contract where it requires you to work wholly or mainly outside the UK. Instead, it must keep a memorandum showing your name and the duration of the contract. Where your contract is with a subsidiary company, the memorandum must give the name of that subsidiary.

Your company must notify the Registrar of Companies of where the copies or memorandum are kept, unless they are kept at the registered office. Shareholders may inspect them free of charge. If inspection is refused the shareholder can go to court and get an order for inspection to be allowed.

WILL THE SHAREHOLDERS HAVE TO APPROVE ANY OF THE TERMS OF MY SERVICE CONTRACT?

In general, no. However, if you want your contract to include a term requiring your company or any of its subsidiaries to employ you for more than five years, so that that term cannot be terminated, then that term must be approved *beforehand* by ordinary resolution of the shareholders in a general meeting (see page 82). The law contains complicated provisions to deal with variations on this theme, for example, to cover the situation where you may already be employed under such a contract before appointment as a director.

Where shareholders' approval is required, a written memorandum setting out the *whole* of the proposed contract must be made available for the shareholders to inspect for fifteen days before that meeting and at the meeting itself.

Should your contract inadvertently have been entered into without such approval, it will still be valid. However, the term providing for its duration will not be valid. The law then 'deems' your contract to include a term entitling the company to terminate your contract on giving reasonable notice. What is meant by 'reasonable' is not defined. It is unlikely, however, to exceed three months.

WILL MY NAME APPEAR ON THE COMPANY NOTEPAPER?

There is no longer any legal requirement that the names of a company's directors should appear on its business correspondence. However, where a company incorporated on or after 23 November 1916 states the name of *any* director on its business correspondence, it must go on to state clearly the surname and christian name (or initials) of *all* its directors. Where a director is a company, its corporate name must be given.

I'VE BEEN ASKED BY THE COMPANY'S BANKERS TO GIVE A GUARANTEE OF ITS BANK OVERDRAFT. SHOULD I?

Frequently, a personal guarantee will be the only way of the company obtaining finance, particularly when an existing business is incorporated for the first time. However, there is always a risk that if your business is unsuccessful your company may become insolvent. In this event you will be liable on the guarantee you have given. Furthermore, such a guarantee may involve placing a charge on your family home, which you could risk losing if the guarantee was enforced.

You should always give very careful consideration to the risks entailed in giving a personal guarantee. You should see your solicitor and ask him to run through the terms of the guarantee with you, for example, the extent and duration of the guarantee and how and when it can be enforced. You should see your accountant to discuss with him the future prospects of your business (and, in particular, its cash requirements), and hence whether the finance you have obtained will prove to be adequate.

3. YOUR FUNCTIONS AS A DIRECTOR

Page

What powers do I have as a director? 38

Can I delegate any of my powers? 38

When can I enter into contracts on my company's behalf? 38

Should I sign contracts in my own name or in the company's? 39

Should I sign all cheques? 39

Am I entitled to look at any of the company's records? 39

Can I appoint someone to act in my place, say, if I will be abroad
for a few months? 40

How far can I trust what my employees do without checking
their work myself? 40

I've been asked to be the company's 'Managing Director'. What
does that mean? 41

Are there any formalities to being appointed a Managing
Director? 41

3. YOUR FUNCTIONS AS A DIRECTOR

WHAT POWERS DO I HAVE AS A DIRECTOR?

The Articles of Association of your company will describe a great many powers that relate to the management of the company and its directors. However, they will probably not make clear the position of individual directors. The variety of structures adopted in practice for company boards makes it unlikely that any standard set of rules applicable to all directors could be devised (for example, because of the distinction between executive and non-executive directors). Table A permits the board to appoint a managing director or other executive directors and for the board to delegate its powers on any basis it chooses to a committee. Since a committee can be represented by a single director then the board may delegate any of its powers to that director. The only powers you have, therefore, as a director are those delegated to you by the board.

CAN I DELEGATE ANY OF MY POWERS?

There seems to be no reason why not. However, where you do delegate any of your powers, you still remain responsible for their exercise. Therefore, it is always good practice to confirm what you are delegating in writing to the manager or other members of staff concerned.

WHEN CAN I ENTER INTO CONTRACTS ON MY COMPANY'S BEHALF?

You can bind the company to any contract which would normally be within the powers of a director of your type. If you are a Managing Director you can bind the company to any contract which is in the ordinary course of your company's business. Your company will be bound even if you have not been delegated power to enter that type of contract by your board. This stems from the legal rule laid down in the case of *Royal British Bank v. Turquard* (1856) 6 E&B 327 that a person dealing with a company in good faith is entitled, in the absence of some indication to the contrary, to assume that the company has complied with all matters of internal procedure necessary for it to enter a valid contract. However, the contract must still be within the *company's* power to enter into as defined by its objects clause (see page 5).

SHOULD I SIGN CONTRACTS IN MY OWN NAME OR IN THE COMPANY'S?

When you enter into a contract on your company's behalf, you are acting as its agent. It is important, therefore, that this agency is clearly established or otherwise you will risk being personally liable on the contract. Usually it is sufficient if you sign 'for' or 'on behalf of' your company, particularly if the context makes it clear that you intended to contract as agent of your company. It will help in making this clear if you carry out all correspondence on your company's headed letter paper and also if you describe yourself as 'Mr X, Sales Director' or as appropriate. Where large or unusual contracts are concerned you would be wise to take professional advice.

SHOULD I SIGN ALL CHEQUES?

This will depend upon whose names are on the bank mandate. Commonly, this may be the directors only, particularly where the company has grown quickly from being owned/managed by the directors. Usually, it is possible for an arrangement to be made with your company's bank whereby specified individuals can be delegated responsibility for signing cheques up to a certain amount. Alternatively, mechanical cheque signing arrangements can be devised where the volume of cheques is substantial. In a large company it may not be appropriate for a director to sign all cheques relating to his area of responsibility personally. It is also better management to delegate responsibility down the chain of command as far as is practicable, provided that, in this instance, suitable controls over the cheque signatories are introduced.

One matter you should be careful of is that the company name is accurately described on any cheque or order. If it is not accurately described you will not only be personally liable on it if the company does not honour it, but also you will be personally liable on summary conviction to a maximum fine of £400.

AM I ENTITLED TO LOOK AT ANY OF THE COMPANY'S RECORDS?

You have a statutory right to inspect your company's accounting records. Case law makes it clear that you may inspect the company's statutory books, but it is not clear what else you are entitled to see. You should be able to see any records that you need to carry out your own duties, or that are relevant to ascertaining whether any statutory obligation has been fulfilled that you as a company officer could be liable for if breached. Otherwise the answer to this question seems to be no. If a matter does concern you, the appropriate forum to raise it is at a board meeting.

CAN I APPOINT SOMEONE TO ACT IN MY PLACE, SAY, IF I WILL BE ABROAD FOR A FEW MONTHS?

Yes. You can appoint an 'alternate' director (see page 28).

HOW FAR CAN I TRUST WHAT MY EMPLOYEES DO WITHOUT CHECKING THEIR WORK MYSELF?

The extent of your duties are considered below in Chapter 4. The basic proposition stated there (see page 43) is that:

> In respect of all duties that, having regard to the exigencies of business, and the articles of association, may properly be left to some other official, a director is, in the absence of grounds for suspicion, justified in trusting that official to perform such duties honestly.

This has been put well in another case where *Lord Halsbury LC* said in relation to the directors of a bank:

> I cannot think that it can be expected of a director that he should be watching either the inferior officers of the bank or verifying the calculations of the auditors himself. The business of life could not go on if people could not trust those who are put into a position of trust for the express purpose of attending to details of management. [*Davey v. Cary* [1901] AC 477].

You should bear in mind, however, that if you are in an executive role, a court is more likely to find that you had grounds for suspicion or were negligent in trusting a particular official than in these cases. This is because these cases date back to the turn of the century and earlier, and reflect the different appreciation of a director's role and responsibilities. It is recommended, therefore, that a system is introduced to ensure that there is effective control over the actions of company officials.

I'VE BEEN ASKED TO BE THE COMPANY'S
'MANAGING DIRECTOR'. WHAT DOES THAT MEAN?

Precisely what powers you will have as a Managing Director will depend on the powers delegated to you by your board or given to you in your service contract. People outside the company can assume that you have the power to enter into contracts of *any type* on your company's behalf. Hence, you will be able to bind your company in respect of contracts of any type. This is in contrast to the position of, for example, a Finance Director, who can only bind his company in respect of those contracts which it is normal for a Finance Director to enter into.

In addition, as a Managing Director you will not be required to retire by rotation (see page 110).

ARE THERE ANY FORMALITIES TO BEING
APPOINTED A MANAGING DIRECTOR?

First, the Articles of Association of your company must specifically entitle the board to delegate its powers to a Managing Director. Table A does so.

Secondly, you must be formally appointed by the board. The powers to be delegated to you should be specifically approved and the fact of your appointment must be noted in the board minutes.

4. YOUR DUTIES AS A DIRECTOR TO YOUR COMPANY

Page

To whom am I responsible as a director? 43

I know that my company is about to enter into a contract with a
company in which I own shares. Do I need to do anything? 45

Can I get around this by entering into an arrangement with the
company I own rather than a legally binding contract? 45

When do I have to disclose my interest? 45

Can I vote on a contract in which I have declared an interest? 45

My company enters into a large number of such contracts. Do I
have to go through this procedure every time? 46

What happens if I don't disclose my interest in a contract? 46

Will only the board know of such contracts? 46

Is that all? 46

What happens if these procedures are not followed? 47

I am a director of a Stock Exchange listed company. Are there
any additional requirements I must satisfy? 47

My company has had to turn down a contract because it has too
much work. Can I take it on personally? 49

Can my company exempt me from or indemnify me against any
liability I incur as a director? 49

Can I insure against being liable as a director? 49

4. YOUR DUTIES AS A DIRECTOR TO YOUR COMPANY

TO WHOM AM I RESPONSIBLE AS A DIRECTOR?

Your company

The law lays three main duties upon company directors to their company, that is, to its shareholders. These are general duties, applicable in all circumstances. In addition, Parliament has laid down specific duties that company directors owe to their company. These are considered later in this chapter. The three main general duties are that a director has a duty to care for his company, called 'the duty of care', which is relatively light, a more onerous 'fiduciary duty', which is to act *bona fide* in the interests of their company, and a strict duty to act only within his powers as a director.

- Your duty of care

  The traditional view of the standard of care which a director is expected to show to his company was stated by *Romer J.* in *Re City Equitable Fire Insurance Co. Ltd.* [1925] Ch 407, and can be summarised in the following way:

  - A director need not show a greater degree of skill than may reasonably be expected from a person of his knowledge and experience. Directors are not liable for mere errors of judgement.
  - A director does not have to give continuous attention to the affairs of his company. His duties are of an intermittent nature to be performed at periodical board meetings, and at meetings of any committee of the board upon which he happens to be placed. He does not, however, have to attend all such meetings, although he should do so, whenever, in the circumstances, he is reasonably able to do so.
  - A director is entitled to trust company officials to perform their duties honestly, where those duties can properly be left to them and in the absence of grounds for suspicion.

The second statement is probably still true as it applies to non-executive directors. However, since 1925 it has become almost invariable practice for full-time executive directors and managing directors to be appointed. Such directors must almost certainly be under a duty to give continuous attention to their company's affairs. Consequently, the standard of care that they should exercise would also be increased to take account of their greater involvement and knowledge of the company's affairs.

43

- Your fiduciary duty

  Directors must act '*bona fide* in what they consider – not what a court may consider – is in the interests of the company, and not for any collateral purpose'. [*Lord Greene MR* in *Re. Smith and Fawcett Ltd* [1942] Ch 304.]

  To be regarded as acting *bona fide* in the interests of your company, you must act in accordance with what you perceive to be the best interests of the company's shareholders. It was once the case that this duty was so strict that *ex gratia* payments to employees could be construed as contrary to the interests of a company. This is now reversed, and the *Companies Act 1985* provides that the directors of a company must have regard to the interests of its employees in general as well as shareholders. It is another way of saying that directors must not act for any collateral purpose, for example, any ulterior motive. However, acting for a collateral purpose will not always be against the best interests of a company, and so shareholders can authorise such an act in general meeting, provided that it does not constitute a fraud upon any minority of shareholders.

- Your duty to act within your powers

  As a director, you must not do anything which is outside the powers of your company as laid down in the objects clause of its Memorandum of Association (see page 5). Nor must you do anything which goes beyond the powers conferred upon you as a director by your company's Articles of Association (see page 6), unless the shareholders expressly approve it. If you were to do such an act and your company suffered a loss as a consequence, it would be entitled to recover the amount of the loss from you personally.

Your employees

As mentioned above, a company's directors are now under a legal duty to have regard to the interests of their employees. Although this is a good statement of principle, there are no legal teeth by which employees can enforce it, as the obligation is owed to the company and not to its employees. However, any successful business will be only too aware that its most important assets are its employees, and it fails to consider their interests at its own peril. Furthermore, directors will need some awareness of their legal responsibilities to employees, for example, regarding health and safety at work. These obligations are considered in outline in Chapter 6.

Your customers

A company will survive and grow only if it satisfies its customers. Even large monopolistic institutions cannot ignore this indefinitely. Besides this 'commercial' duty to customers, directors should make themselves aware of the basis of consumer law and any provisions relating to their particular industry.

I KNOW THAT MY COMPANY IS ABOUT TO ENTER INTO A CONTRACT WITH A COMPANY IN WHICH I OWN SHARES. DO I NEED TO DO ANYTHING?

As a director, or a shadow director, you must disclose to the board the nature of any direct or indirect interest you or a person connected with you (as defined later on page 93) have in any contract or proposed contract with your company (see below).

CAN I GET AROUND THIS BY ENTERING INTO AN ARRANGEMENT WITH THE COMPANY I OWN RATHER THAN A LEGALLY BINDING CONTRACT?

No. Those who drafted the legislation foresaw this possibility and 'contract' includes, for this purpose, any transaction or arrangement, whether or not constituting a contract.

WHEN DO I HAVE TO DISCLOSE MY INTEREST?

As soon as a contract is proposed, you should declare your interest at the first board meeting where the question of entering into the contract is considered. Where your interest arises only after a contract has been proposed or made, you should declare your interest at the next board meeting, whether or not that contract is to be considered.

CAN I VOTE ON A CONTRACT IN WHICH I HAVE DECLARED AN INTEREST?

The law and the new Table A do not prohibit you from voting. However, it is probably best practice if you do not.

If your company adopted the old Table A and has not amended it, you are prohibited from voting in respect of any contract or arrangement in which you are 'interested'. Furthermore, your vote (if you attempt to exercise it) must not be counted and your presence does not count towards the *quorum* for the meeting (see page 52). There are limited exceptions to this, the most important of these is where your interest arises only because you are a shareholder. In any event, the old

Table A provides that your company's shareholders in a general meeting can at any time suspend or relax the prohibition *generally* or in respect of any particular contract.

It is very common for companies to adopt their own provisions in respect of directors' interests in contracts and you should check the particular Articles of Association of your company.

MY COMPANY ENTERS INTO A LARGE NUMBER OF SUCH CONTRACTS. DO I HAVE TO GO THROUGH THIS PROCEDURE EVERY TIME?

No. You can give a general notice to the board either to the effect that:

- You are a member of a specified company or firm and you are to be regarded as interested in any contract which may, after the date of the notice, be made with that company or firm, or
- You are to be regarded as interested in any contract which may, after the date of the notice, be made with a connected person (as defined later on page 93).

WHAT HAPPENS IF I DON'T DISCLOSE MY INTEREST IN A CONTRACT?

Firstly, you are liable to be fined. On trial on indictment the fine is unlimited – on summary trial it is limited to a maximum of £2,000. Furthermore, a court might subsequently take the view that entering into the contract was in breach of your fiduciary duty to your company (see page 119).

WILL ONLY THE BOARD KNOW OF SUCH CONTRACTS?

If you have a material interest in a contract it will have to be disclosed in your company's financial statements. It is for the board to decide on whether a transaction is material or not. The details of what disclosures are required are considered on page 99.

IS THAT ALL?

No. There are further legal restrictions upon a company entering into what are called 'substantial property transactions' involving a director, who for this purpose includes persons connected with him and shadow directors.

A company is prohibited from entering into an 'arrangement' with a director to acquire from, or transfer to, the company a non-cash asset, except in the following circumstances:

- The shareholders approve it in advance in general meeting.
- The shareholders affirm it within a reasonable period.
- The value of the non-cash asset is less than £1,000 or, if it is greater, the lower of £50,000 or 10% of the company's net assets.
- It is between a wholly-owned subsidiary and either its holding company or a fellow wholly-owned subsidiary.
- It is with a company which is being wound up (except by a members' voluntary winding up).
- The director is acquiring a non-cash asset in his capacity as a member of the company.

WHAT HAPPENS IF THESE PROCEDURES ARE NOT FOLLOWED?

The company is entitled to treat the arrangement as void, unless one of the following applies:

- It is no longer possible for the cash or property involved to be restored to the company.
- A third party has in good faith given value to acquire rights which would be affected.

Furthermore, in this type of situation, you will be liable to account to the company for any gain you may have made as a result and to indemnify the company for any loss or damage it may suffer.

I AM A DIRECTOR OF A STOCK EXCHANGE LISTED COMPANY. ARE THERE ANY ADDITIONAL REQUIREMENTS I MUST SATISFY?

Yes. These are contained in The Stock Exchange's Yellow Book, which is the colloquial name given to the 'Admission of Securities to Listing' because of its colour. This sets out the rules that companies applying to be listed on The Stock Exchange must follow in making their application and various continuing obligations upon them afterwards. The Yellow Book sets out rules which apply where a company proposes to enter into what is termed a 'Class 4' transaction.

A Class 4 transaction is any transaction of a capital nature between a director or associate of his and his company. 'Associate' in this respect has a similar meaning to a 'connected person' in company law (see page 93). Examples of Class 4 transactions include, but are not confined to:

- An acquisition or disposal of assets by a company to a director or his associate.
- A transaction, whose principal purpose or effect is to lend money, grant credit to or guarantee the loan of a director or his associate. However, the granting of credit on normal commercial terms in the ordinary and usual course of business is *excluded* to avoid the rules applying, for example, to retail charge cards.

If your company proposes to enter into any transaction which may be a Class 4 transaction it is essential that at an early stage you discuss this with its broker. He will then be able to consult The Stock Exchange's Quotations Department to establish whether compliance with the requirements for Class 4 transactions will be necessary. The Quotations Committee will normally require your company to send a 'circular' to its shareholders and seek the consent of the company's shareholders in a general meeting. When you are a shareholder as well as a director, you may be required to abstain from voting at that general meeting and this must be stated in the circular.

You should note that The Stock Exchange has, for some time, accepted that, where a Class 4 transaction is small relative to the company concerned, it will not require that the shareholders should approve the transaction. However, this concession will apply only if the company sets out information covering the transaction in its next annual report, and if the Quotations Department of The Stock Exchange receives a letter from the company's auditors (or, sometimes, other advisers) stating that, in their opinion, the terms of the transaction are fair and reasonable so far as the company's shareholders are concerned. In all such cases The Stock Exchange should still be consulted beforehand.

The size test below which The Stock Exchange may make this concession are generally 1% as regards main board directors, 2% as regards a subsidiary company's directors (carried out by comparing the consideration given or received with the company's net tangible assets), or an amount of consideration less than £20,000.

Where a circular must be sent to your shareholders, your brokers or other professional advisors should be consulted over its content. Generally speaking, the circular should aim to demonstrate the reasonableness and fairness of the proposed transaction and must make the balance of advantage or disadvantage to the company readily apparent, to enable a shareholder to reach his own conclusion on the proposal.

MY COMPANY HAS HAD TO TURN DOWN A CONTRACT BECAUSE IT HAS TOO MUCH WORK. CAN I TAKE IT ON PERSONALLY?

Yes. However, you may only do so if you fully disclose all the information which is relevant about the contract to your board first. If the board, in good faith, decides to turn down the opportunity, you may take the contract on personally, provided that no term of your service contract prohibits this. It is recommended in such circumstances that the board minutes its reasons for rejecting the opportunity, to show that it was done in good faith just in case this was to be challenged at a later date . One example where the decision could be in good faith is where the company cannot do the work itself.

CAN MY COMPANY EXEMPT ME FROM OR INDEMNIFY ME AGAINST ANY LIABILITY I INCUR AS A DIRECTOR?

Your company cannot alter its Articles of Association, or put a term in your service contract, so as to exempt or indemnify you against any liability you may suffer for negligence, breach of duty or breach of trust which you may commit against it. The law provides that any such term would be void. The only exception to this is that your company can agree to indemnify you in respect of the costs of defending civil or criminal proceedings that you win.

There is, however, a loophole in the law. If you are a director of a subsidiary company, that company's holding company or a fellow subsidiary can exempt you or indemnify you for such liabilities.

CAN I INSURE AGAINST BEING LIABLE AS A DIRECTOR?

You can insure against most forms of civil action that may be taken against you. In fact, this is increasingly common in practice. However, bear in mind that some forms of civil action, such as for libel and slander, and all forms of criminal proceedings, will usually be uninsurable.

You will usually have to bear the cost of such insurance personally. Since a company cannot itself indemnify you, it is very unlikely that it can legally pay premiums on an insurance policy to indemnify you.

Despite the cost, it is recommended that all directors take out such insurance. Even a relatively small claim, in commercial terms, can be ruinous if it has to be borne personally by a director (not least because of the associated legal costs).

5. YOUR DUTIES TO YOUR CO-DIRECTORS

Page

Do directors need to hold regular meetings? 52

How many directors need to attend a board meeting? 52

Where should a board meeting be held? 52

What notice should be given beforehand? 53

Who should be given notice? 54

What should the notice contain? 54

Should there be a chairman of a board meeting? 54

What questions need to be dealt with at a board meeting? 55

What majority is needed for board decisions? 55

Must I attend board meetings? 55

Can I be excluded from any board meeting? 56

The directors of our company are spread throughout the UK and
    some abroad. Can we avoid having a formal board meeting? ... 56

We seem to cover a lot of routine business at board meetings.
    Can we appoint committees to deal with these? 56

Do minutes of board meetings need to be taken? 57

What should be recorded in the minutes? 57

How should minutes be kept? 57

Does anyone need to sign the minutes? 58

What use are the minutes? 58

What can I do if I disagree with the minutes? 58

Am I entitled to see the minutes? 58

Who else can see the minutes? 59

5. YOUR DUTIES TO YOUR CO-DIRECTORS

DO DIRECTORS NEED TO HOLD REGULAR MEETINGS?

It may be a surprise to you that there is no legal requirement even for large public companies to hold board meetings. Table A is representative of most companies' Articles of Association when it provides that 'subject to the provisions of the articles, the directors may regulate their procedings as they think fit'. The procedure for meetings is regulated, but there is no duty to hold any meetings at all. In practice, small private companies will often have no need for formal meetings and larger companies will establish their own non-legal framework for meetings to suit their commercial needs. Despite this, it is a good discipline even for the smallest company to establish a framework for holding board meetings, particularly in the light of the new insolvency legislation (see Chapters 12 and 14).

HOW MANY DIRECTORS NEED TO ATTEND A BOARD MEETING?

Table A provides that the directors may fix the *quorum* of directors necessary to do business at a meeting. A *quorum* is the number of people who must be present at a meeting for it to be validly held. A *quorum* is fixed at two directors unless the directors decide to change this number. An alternate director counts towards the *quorum* provided that the director who appointed him is not also present at the meeting.

Directors should take care that they maintain a *quorum* at a meeting. If, for example, you have a material interest in a matter, Table A does not permit you to vote on it and, furthermore, you will not count towards the *quorum*. This could happen where you have entered into a contract that conflicts with the interests of your company. No one knows what precisely is meant by 'material', in this respect, and it is best to err on the side of caution (see page 45). If this reduces the number of directors below the *quorum*, the continuing director(s) can only act to appoint additional directors to call a general meeting of the company. The company in general meeting then has the power to remove the prohibition on the director acting.

WHERE SHOULD A BOARD MEETING BE HELD?

There are no legal restrictions on where a board meeting should be held. This is a matter which is rightly left to the convenience of the directors. Accordingly, there is no reason why a board meeting should not be held outside the country if, for example, a director considers that entering the UK would have adverse personal tax consequences. Technically, a problem might arise because a director absent from the UK is not entitled under Table A to notice of a meeting. However, in practice notice can always be given. In any event, the Articles of Association can be altered should this rule be inconvenient, but you should seek professional advice on how to do this.

A question which often arises in practice is 'can a meeting be held by telephone?'. The answer seems to be 'yes', provided that provision for this is put in the company's Articles of Association. Table A contains no such provision, and the provisions regarding notice would be highly inconvenient to holding a meeting by telephone. Professional advice should be sought over this question, however, as in some countries the Courts have held that a telephone conversation cannot in law constitute a meeting. The English Courts do not appear to have considered the question.

WHAT NOTICE SHOULD BE GIVEN BEFOREHAND?

Table A does not lay down any specific requirement for notice of a meeting to be given. It simply says that any director may call a meeting at any time and the company secretary must do so at his request. This does not mean that no notice at all will suffice. The length of notice given must be reasonable, having regard to the practice of the company and other surrounding circumstances.

It is possible then for an informal and short notice to suffice in the case of a small company where all the directors are in close touch with each other. In contrast, written notice will almost inevitably be necessary in the case of a large company. This is not to say that inadequate notice will suffice in small companies. *Barron v. Potter* [1915] 3 KB 39 was a case involving two directors who met at Paddington Station. One formally proposed the election of three directors and the other objected. The Court held that this was not a valid meeting.

Where the notice given for a directors' meeting is unreasonable the meeting will be 'void' in legal terms. This means that it will be treated as if it had never taken place at all. Furthermore, any business conducted at the meeting will also be void. However, one point emerges from both the cases mentioned above – a director who is aggrieved must register his objection at the first possible opportunity.

WHO SHOULD BE GIVEN NOTICE?

Notice should be given to *all* the directors. Otherwise there is a risk that the meeting will be 'void'. The one exception to this provided for in Table A is that notice need not be given to a director who is absent from the UK. There is some doubt in legal circles whether it is necessary for a director who is not entitled to vote at a meeting, for some reason, to be given notice. In practice, it is best to give such a director notice. If it is desired that a director should not even speak at a meeting, the appropriate procedure may be to seek his removal from the board – not to seek his exclusion from meetings.

WHAT SHOULD THE NOTICE CONTAIN?

In contrast to the notice given of a shareholders' meeting, there are no requirements as to the contents of the notice to be given to directors. In particular, there is no need to state what business is intended to be transacted at the meeting. Clearly, this procedure may be appropriate for small companies, where a degree of flexibility is necessary and the directors are aware of the affairs of the company as a whole. However, it would be highly inappropriate for there to be no indication on the board agenda given to the directors of a substantial national or international company. In such companies, for board meetings to serve a useful purpose, there should be circulated as a minimum an agenda of proposed business to be transacted. In addition, background papers should be circulated in advance of the meeting, so that an informed decision on important issues affecting the company can be made. This is of particular value where the company has non-executive directors. Unless a non-executive director is well informed he cannot make an effective contribution to the affairs of a company. As noted above, it is a good discipline for even the smallest company to hold board meetings. Such companies are equally recommended to follow the practice adopted by large companies.

SHOULD THERE BE A CHAIRMAN OF A BOARD MEETING?

Table A permits the directors of a company to appoint a chairman to the board of directors. The chairman must then preside at every board meeting he attends unless he is unwilling to do so. In that case, or if he is not present at a meeting within five minutes of its commencement, the directors present may elect another chairman for that meeting.

There is, therefore, no legal requirement for there to be a chairman, although practically speaking it is very useful so that meetings are conducted in an efficient manner. A further incentive to appoint a chairman is given in Table A which provides that where the board cannot reach a decision because there is an equality of votes, the chairman has a second (or 'casting') vote.

WHAT QUESTIONS NEED TO BE DEALT WITH AT A BOARD MEETING?

Company law does not provide that directors may transact the business of the company only at board meetings. To do so would be impracticable. A company should deal with those questions at board meetings which require the combined experience and skills of the whole board, for example, considering the strategy of the company. There is little commercial sense in having valuable board members' time wasted by requiring them to attend a meeting purely, for example, for routine cheque-signing. This is not to say that there is no value in the whole board of a large company exercising a supervisory role over the company's affairs – the Guinness affair has highlighted this. However, board committees including both executive and non-executive directors are more suited to deal with more routine matters, provided that the committees are required to report regularly to the board.

As discussed above (see page 45), in certain circumstances directors must disclose any interest they might have in a company contract to the board, so clearly this is one question which must be dealt with at board meetings.

WHAT MAJORITY IS NEEDED FOR BOARD DECISIONS?

Table A provides that questions arising at any meeting of directors should be decided on a simple majority of votes. Where there is a deadlock, the chairman has a second (or casting vote). In calculating the majority needed you should bear in mind that in certain circumstances (see page 45) some directors may not be entitled to vote. You should also check the Articles of Association of your company to ensure that there is no special provision giving a particular director weighted voting rights.

MUST I ATTEND BOARD MEETINGS?

In legal terms the need for you to attend board meetings will depend on the circumstances, for example, the number of directors on the board and your own role as a director. As a director, you have a general duty to attend board meetings when you can, but you need not attend all of them. Although it is rare for a director to be sued for negligence, if you failed to attend most board meetings, you could certainly be at risk from such an allegation. The only other sanction for non-attendance is provided in Table A, which provides that a director loses his office if he misses meetings for six consecutive months without board permission *and* the directors vote to remove him.

In practical terms, when you accept appointment as a director, you take on responsibilities, one of these is the attendance at board meetings. Particularly in a larger company and if you possess a special skill, say as a Finance Director, then your attendance at board meetings should be an important part of the decision making process. It also answers the need for a formal cross-fertilisation of ideas within a company, which can be a vital element in the formulation of company strategy.

You should also remember that it is courteous to submit your apologies for your absence in advance of the meeting (where it is unavoidable) and to give reasons for this.

CAN I BE EXCLUDED FROM ANY BOARD MEETING?

No. Ultimately it is the shareholders of a company who decide who is to be a director, and it would be wrong if their wishes could be frustrated by a director being excluded from a board meeting. A director who is wrongfully excluded in this way can go to Court and seek an injunction restraining further exclusion.

THE DIRECTORS OF OUR COMPANY ARE SPREAD THROUGHOUT THE UK AND SOME ABROAD. CAN WE AVOID HAVING A FORMAL BOARD MEETING?

In some circumstances, you may be able to hold a valid board meeting by telephone (see page 53). If you need a resolution to be agreed, Table A provides that a resolution signed by all the directors has the same validity as if it had been passed at a meeting.

WE SEEM TO COVER A LOT OF ROUTINE BUSINESS AT BOARD MEETINGS. CAN WE APPOINT COMMITTEES TO DEAL WITH THESE?

Yes. As mentioned above, Table A empowers a board to delegate any of its powers to a committee of one or more directors. The board can also appoint any person to be its agent and, therefore, to exercise any of the powers the directors possess. Your company's board has various options, therefore:

- It can appoint a committee of directors that can only make recommendations to the board, leaving the board to make the final decisions.
- It can appoint a committee or agent to exercise the powers of the board without further reference to it.
- It can appoint a committee of directors to exercise a supervisory or reporting function. One increasingly important example of this in large companies is the 'audit committee'.

DO MINUTES OF BOARD MEETINGS NEED TO BE TAKEN?

Yes. The *Companies Act 1985* requires minutes to be kept of all directors' meetings and meetings of managers. Furthermore, Table A requires there to be a record of the proceedings at all directors' meetings.

WHAT SHOULD BE RECORDED IN THE MINUTES?

Although Table A refers to a record of 'proceedings', no one would expect the minutes to record details of the discussions at a meeting. Rather they are a record of the actual decisions taken. The writing of good minutes of meetings is an art. It requires conciseness, accuracy, objectivity and the absence of any ambiguity.

HOW SHOULD MINUTES BE KEPT?

Responsibility for the keeping of minutes usually falls on the company secretary although this is not a legal requirement. In practice, any person attending a meeting can be asked to take the minutes of it and an ordinary secretary can be invited to attend for this purpose. The minutes must be entered in 'books kept for that purpose'.

There is no requirement that the minute books must be kept in any particular place nor that anyone can inspect them. If the minutes are not properly kept both the company and every officer of it will be liable to a fine of £200, and, for continued contravention, to a daily default fine of £20.

DOES ANYONE NEED TO SIGN THE MINUTES?

No. Although the *Companies Act 1985* provides that a minute signed by the chairman of a meeting or the next succeeding meeting is evidence of the proceedings at that meeting, there is no legal requirement that anyone should sign them.

Contrary to common belief there is no need for the board to confirm or adopt the minutes of a previous meeting, although it is doubtlessly good practice. If the directors approve the minutes of a meeting in some way it will be difficult subsequently for a director to deny his collective responsibility for any decision.

WHAT USE ARE THE MINUTES?

As noted above, minutes signed by the chairman are evidence of the proceedings at a meeting. The *Companies Act 1985* does not, however, deem them to be conclusive evidence of what has happened at a meeting, although there is nothing to prevent the company's Articles of Association from containing such a provision. Therefore, if a matter to which the minutes relate should ever come before a court, it is possible to submit alternative evidence to show that the minutes are incomplete or inaccurate.

WHAT CAN I DO IF I DISAGREE WITH THE MINUTES?

You should state your objection at the first possible opportunity. However, you are at the mercy of the chairman (if he takes responsibility for the minutes) as to whether or not your objection is formally recorded. If that happens, you would be wise to consider some other documentary means of recording your objection, and depending on the seriousness of the matter, you may also need to seek professional advice.

AM I ENTITLED TO SEE THE MINUTES?

There is no statutory right that entitles you to see them, nor any right in Table A. However, the Courts recognise the need for a director to be able to see minutes of board meetings as he may be called to account for matters included in them. Consequently, at common law you have the right to see the minutes.

WHO ELSE CAN SEE THE MINUTES?

The auditors of your company have a statutory right of access to the company's books and this includes board minutes. However, a company's shareholders and other persons do not have that right.

6. YOUR RESPONSIBILITIES TO YOUR EMPLOYEES

Page

Who exactly are my company's employees? 61

Are there any rules on how staff can be recruited? 61

What are the formalities involved in employing a person? 63

Can my company pay its employees by cheque or must it pay by
cash? 65

Can my company make any deductions from employees' wages? . 65

Do I have to pay my employees if they are ill? 65

What happens if an employee becomes pregnant? 66

Are my employees entitled to holiday pay? 66

What are my responsibilities for my employees' health and safety
at work? 67

What if my employees belong to a trade union? 67

How does the sex and race discrimination legislation affect my
company? 68

Can I take on foreign employees? 69

How do I dismiss a person? 69

What sort of 'notice' is necessary? 70

When is a dismissal 'unfair'? 70

6. YOUR RESPONSIBILITIES TO YOUR EMPLOYEES

WHO EXACTLY ARE MY COMPANY'S EMPLOYEES?

Usually you will not need to ask this question because the answer will be obvious. However, if, for example, your company operates in the construction or clothing sectors, you may need to consider whether or not the people who work for you should be employed or self-employed. The distinction is not just of academic interest. If a person performs work for you as an employee, he will be entitled to a wide variety of statutory rights and you will owe him corresponding duties. Your only duties to the self-employed are to act in accordance with your contract, provide him with a safe place and system of work and not to practice sexual or racial discrimination. Furthermore, the operation of the taxation system applies differently for the employed and self-employed.

There are a number of factors that the Courts and Industrial Tribunals take into account when they need to decide whether a person is an employee or is self-employed. The important point to remember is that you cannot get out of your legal obligations to an employee simply by calling him 'self-employed'. It is the substance of the relationship and not its form that the courts will look at.

A person can only be an employee if you are obliged under a contract to provide him with work and he is obliged to perform it. Once that condition is satisfied, it is possible for a person to be viewed as an employee. Other factors to be considered are of differing importance. For example, does the company control not only what the person does, but also how and when he must do it? Is his work part of your business? Does he provide his own equipment and his own assistants? What is his financial involvement in his work? Does he receive a salary, sick pay or paid holidays? Is he allowed to work for other companies? No one item is conclusive. If the establishment or otherwise of an employment relationship is of particular importance to you, you should consider taking professional advice *before* recruiting your staff or contracting for self-employed staff.

ARE THERE ANY RULES ON HOW STAFF CAN BE RECRUITED?

Yes, lots.

- Recruitment advertising
  Advertisements must not show any intention to unlawfully

discriminate by sex. There is a similar prohibition against discrimination by race. However, where sex or race is a genuine occupational qualification for a job, discrimination may be acceptable. For example, you can lawfully advertise for Indian waiters for an Indian restaurant. On the other hand, you cannot use job descriptions with a particular connotation, for example, 'sales girl' would need to be replaced by 'sales assistant'.

- Interviewing and selection
  You are not allowed to discriminate by sex or race in your arrangements for deciding who should be offered an interview. Furthermore, you are not allowed to require information to be given on an application form or to ask questions at an interview in respect of certain past criminal convictions. However, you can discriminate on other grounds. For example, employers may wish to discriminate in favour of non-smokers.

- Offers of employment
  You are not allowed to discriminate by sex or race either by refusing or deliberately omitting to offer a person employment or in the terms of employment that you offer a person.

- The disabled
  First, anyone who wishes to employ a lift or car park attendant *must* employ 'a disabled person' as defined in statute.

  Secondly, if you employ a 'substantial number' of employees you *must* employ a quota of 3% of disabled persons or be liable to a fine and/or imprisonment. The quota is 0.1% for employment on British ships.

  Thirdly, if your company employs on average, more than 250 employees in the UK each week during its financial year, the Directors' Report must contain a statement that describes the company's policy during the year in respect of the following:

  - Giving full and fair consideration (having regard to the person's particular aptitudes and abilities) to applications for employment from disabled persons.
  - Continuing the employment of, and arranging the appropriate training for, any of the company's employees who have become disabled during the period in which the company employed them.
  - Otherwise providing for the training, the career development and the promotion of those disabled persons the company employs.

WHAT ARE THE FORMALITIES INVOLVED IN EMPLOYING A PERSON?

- References

  When you make an offer of employment it is usual to make the offer 'subject to satisfactory references being obtained'. This provides you with some protection that the person actually has the experience he claims and may also provide you with other valuable information as to whether he will be a good employee. For example, whether he is honest, whether he keeps good time, why he is leaving, whether he has unpleasant personal characteristics. Frequently, employers make use of a standard form to ensure that the matters they are concerned with are covered.

  There are two further advantages to this process. First, you may be required to take up references under the terms of fidelity insurance if your employees regularly handle cash as part of their work. Secondly, you may be able to sue a person who gives a reference negligently.

- The contract of employment

  There is no more need in law for a contract of employment to be in writing than any other type of general contract. You are, however, under a legal duty to give your employees written particulars of certain important terms of their contracts of employment no later than thirteen weeks after the person commenced employment. The main particulars are:

  - The parties to the contract.
  - The date when the employment began.
  - The date on which the employee's period of 'continuous' employment began. This is to take into account any employment with a previous employer which is to count towards that period.
  - The scale, rate or method of calculating pay.
  - The intervals of payment.
  - Any terms and conditions over working hours.
  - Any terms and conditions over holiday entitlement, incapacity for work and pension arrangements.
  - The length of notice, or date of leaving, where it is fixed.
  - The job description.
  - Whether a 'contracting-out certificate' is in force.
  - Details of any disciplinary rules applying to the employee and to whom the employee can go if he is dissatisfied with a disciplinary decision or has any other grievance.

The fact that these particulars are required does not mean that you must provide for them in your agreement with an employee. If there is no such term, all you need do is to state that fact in the written statement.

You may be wondering at this point whether the law requires you to give a separate contract of employment to each employee. First, the written statement is *not* the contract of employment with an employee, nor is it even conclusive evidence of it. Secondly, if you do give a written contract of employment to an employee then you do not need to give him the written statement. Thirdly, you can simply give an employee a notice instead, referring him to a document which he has a reasonable opportunity of reading in the course of his job, or which is made readily accessible to him in some other way, and which meets the statutory requirements.

- Itemised pay statements
The law requires that all employers must give their employees a written pay statement before or when wages or salary are paid. This must itemise:

  - The gross amount of the wages or salary.
  - The amount of any deductions and why they are made.
  - The net amount of wages or salary payable.
  - Where the net amount is paid in different ways, the amount and method of each.

One important exception to this rule is where you employ part-time staff. You need not give an itemised pay statement to an employee who is required to work for less than sixteen hours a week, unless he works for eight hours or more, but less than sixteen hours a week, *and* has been employed for five years or more.

- Pay As You Earn (PAYE)
The PAYE system is the statutory system for collecting income tax and national insurance contributions when they are paid by an employer rather than by annual assessment. The Inland Revenue enforces the operation of the PAYE system strictly and investigates suspected breaches. You must ensure that your company complies with the relevant legislation. Full treatment of this important subject is outside the scope of this book. Detailed instructions on the operation of PAYE are contained in the Inland Revenue booklet *Employer's Guide to PAYE* and in *PAYE Survival* (Deloitte Haskins & Sells, 1988).

- Employers' liability insurance

  All employers who carry on business in Great Britain must take out an 'approved' insurance policy with an 'authorised' insurer against liability for injury or disease sustained by employees arising out of and in the course of their employment in Great Britain. The annual insurance certificate must be displayed at every place where the employer carries on business so that it can be easily seen and read by all employees.

CAN MY COMPANY PAY ITS EMPLOYEES BY CHEQUE OR MUST IT PAY BY CASH?

It used to be the case that employers had to pay manual workers in cash unless the person consented to payment by cheque. Since 1 January 1987 all restrictions on how employees may be paid have been removed. It is now a matter to be decided by you and your employee in agreeing upon the terms of the contract of employment.

CAN MY COMPANY MAKE ANY DEDUCTIONS FROM AN EMPLOYEE'S WAGES?

Yes, but only in each of the following situations:

- The deduction is required or permitted under a statutory provision, for example, an attachment of earnings order, PAYE or NI.
- The deduction is required or permitted under the employee's contract of employment – but the employee must have been shown the contract of employment or been notified of its terms first.
- The employee has given his prior written consent.
- The employee is in *retail* employment, in which case you are entitled to deduct up to one-tenth of the gross wages to the employee for a particular pay-day in respect of cash shortages or stock deficiencies provided that you follow a set procedure to notify the employee.

DO I HAVE TO PAY MY EMPLOYEES IF THEY ARE ILL?

Yes. First of all you may have agreed to pay sick pay to employees in your contract of employment with them. Regardless of your private agreement with an employee, subject to certain exceptions, you are liable to pay them 'statutory sick pay' ('SSP'). If you do not make this payment, the employee is entitled to require written reasons for your decision, against which he can appeal before a local tribunal. The most important exceptions from this duty are where the employee's weekly earnings are below the weekly lower earnings limit for National Insurance contribution purposes, or where the employee has been taken on for a specified period of three months or less.

Secondly, you must pay an employee SSP where he is sick for at least four consecutive days (including Sundays and Public Holidays) during which he was too ill to work, has notified you of this and supplied evidence of the sickness. There are various exceptions to this rule, for example, where you pay an employee below the minimum level required to pay National Insurance Contributions. The maximum entitlement to SSP over a three year period is generally twenty-eight weeks, after which an employee must claim state sickness benefit. There are fixed rates of SSP payable, which you can recover from the employee's and employer's National Insurance contributions due for that month or subsequent months. Detailed records relating to SSP must be kept for three years.

You will find the DHSS booklet *Employer's Guide to Statutory Sick Pay* (NI 227) helpful in administering SSP.

WHAT HAPPENS IF AN EMPLOYEE BECOMES PREGNANT?

First, you cannot dismiss her without the dismissal being automatically unfair (see page 70) unless at the date the employment ends she will be incapable of doing her work adequately or cannot continue to work without herself (or you, as her employer) breaking the law in some way. In addition, she will have the right to take time off for ante-natal care and to return to work after her confinement.

Secondly, you will have to pay her 'statutory maternity pay' ('SMP') for eighteen consecutive weeks beginning no earlier than the eleventh week before the expected week of confinement and no later than the sixth week. In most cases you will be able to deduct the SMP you pay from the National Insurance contributions you pay.

You will find the DHSS booklet *Employers' Guide to Statutory Maternity Pay* (NI 257) helpful in administering SMP.

ARE MY EMPLOYEES ENTITLED TO HOLIDAY PAY?

No. This is a matter that will depend on your contract of employment with your employee. Holiday entitlement is one of the matters which must be specified when you employ a person as part of the written particulars of their contract of employment (see page 63). However, it is usual for most employers to pay holiday pay.

WHAT ARE MY RESPONSIBILITIES FOR MY EMPLOYEES' HEALTH AND SAFETY AT WORK?

This is a very complicated subject and there are special regulations governing particular industries and particularly hazardous occupations. The Courts have laid down a wide ranging duty on employers to take care of their employees, for example, in terms of providing employees with a safe place of work. If you are negligent in performing these duties, you may be liable to a claim for damages by your employees (although you are bound to insure against this liability anyway). General legislation bearing upon health and safety are the *Factories Act 1961*, the *Offices, Shops and Railway Premises Act 1963* and the *Health and Safety at Work Act 1974*. In addition, a multitude of regulations govern particular industries.

A feature of the legislation that is of practical daily importance to you is the need to maintain an 'accident book'. All employers with more than ten employees must keep an accident book in which various details may be recorded. All employers who own or occupy a factory (or mine or quarry) must keep such a book regardless of how many employees they have. In addition, employers are under a duty to notify death, certain serious injuries, diseases and incidents to their 'enforcing authority' by the fastest practicable means. This will usually be your local authority or may be the Health and Safety Commission and Executive. Notification must be made in writing on a prescribed form within seven days.

As an employer, you are also required, if you employ five or more employees, to prepare and keep up to date a written statement of your general policy regarding health and safety at work and the organisation and arrangements for carrying out that policy. This must be brought to the attention of all employees and be placed in an accessible position.

Furthermore, in certain circumstances you must give facilities and allow time off for the training of 'safety representatives' appointed by a recognised trade union. Their function is to represent the employees in discussions with you over health and safety arrangements. They will also be involved in investigating potential hazards and complaints.

WHAT IF MY EMPLOYEES BELONG TO A TRADE UNION?

First of all, you owe certain obligations to the trade union and the extent of these may surprise you. The most important are:

- The trade union is entitled to certain collective bargaining information as of right.
- The trade union can demand to be consulted on pending redundancies.
- The trade union can demand to be consulted on a planned transfer of the employer's undertaking.
- The trade union is entitled to appoint safety representatives (see above).

Secondly, individual employees who are members of the trade union will have certain rights that they can enforce against you. The most important are:

- Where an employee is a trade union official, he is entitled to take time off during his working hours to carry out his duties and undergo training and be paid during the time off.
- Where an employee is a trade union member, he is entitled to time off during his working hours to take part in certain trade union activities (excluding industrial action) but he is not entitled to be paid during the time off.
- An employee has a right not to have detrimental action taken against him or to be dismissed for membership of, or taking part in, the activities of a trade union. Where an employee is dismissed for this the dismissal is automatically unfair.

These rights only apply where the trade union is 'independent', a requirement basically that the trade union is not really under the control of the employer. A trade union which is independent will invariably have a certificate from the Certification Officer of Trade Unions to prove this.

HOW DOES THE SEX AND RACE DISCRIMINATION LEGISLATION AFFECT MY COMPANY?

In general terms, you must not discriminate against an employee on the grounds of race or sex in the way that you offer that employee access to opportunities for promotion, transfer or training. This also includes refusing access to any other benefits, facilities or services or by refusing or deliberately omitting to afford him access to them or in the terms of employment afforded him. Nor can you subject an employee to any other detriment on the grounds of race or sex. As with most legal rules you will find that there are exceptions to this. As discussed above (see page 62), an important exception is where race or sex is a 'genuine occupational qualification'. There are many others, however, and if this is an area which concerns you, you should take appropriate professional advice.

CAN I TAKE ON FOREIGN EMPLOYEES?

Yes. However, you and the employees will need to comply with various formalities. The burden of these will depend upon whether the proposed employees are nationals of European Community countries or elsewhere.

- Nationals of European Community member states
  Except for Irish nationals, such persons will need a 'residence permit' if they wish to stay in the UK for more than six months. Obtaining this is the responsibility of the proposed employee and your company will usually not be involved.
- Nationals of other countries
  Such persons require a 'work permit'. If you wish to employ someone in this category you will need to satisfy all of the following conditions:

  - That the person will fall within specified categories of workers, for example, professionally qualified staff, where appropriate.
  - That a genuine vacancy exists.
  - That there is no suitable resident labour. This will require extensive advertising of the post.
  - That the application is for a manual worker for a specific job with a specific employer, where appropriate.
  - That the wages and terms of employment are no less favourable than those prevailing in the area for similar work.

HOW DO I DISMISS A PERSON?

Actually dismissing an employee is very easy. You can give the person the notice they are entitled to, or if they are guilty of gross misconduct (for example, theft) you can dismiss an employee on the spot. The period of notice will normally be that contained in the contract of employment. If you act in breach of the contract of employment, the dismissal will be 'wrongful' and the employee may be entitled to damages for breach of contract. However, whatever the contractual position, the employee is entitled (unless he is guilty of gross misconduct) to a minimum period of notice by statute, which depends upon his length of service. What you need to be concerned with is that you do not dismiss an employee unfairly (see below). If you do, an Industrial Tribunal could well order that the employee be reinstated or be paid compensation.

WHAT SORT OF 'NOTICE' IS NECESSARY?

The actual form of the notice will depend upon what is required in the contract of employment. Usually, any clear written notice will suffice for that purpose. However, the law provides that an employee is entitled to be given a written statement giving details of the reasons for his dismissal if he has been employed for more than six months.

WHEN IS A DISMISSAL 'UNFAIR'?

This is a question which is difficult to answer in general terms. However, to bring a claim for unfair dismissal an employee must first of all show that he has been employed for *at least two years* and been *dismissed*. If, therefore, a person has been employed for less than two years you can dismiss him with little or no difficulty.

Secondly, you will have to show what the principal ground for the dismissal was and that it was because of one of five acceptable grounds. These are:

- That it related to the capability or qualifications of the employee for performing his work.
- That it related to the employee's conduct.
- That the employee was redundant.
- That the employee could not have continued to work in that position without breaking the law in some way.
- That it was for 'some other substantial reason of a kind such as to justify the dismissal'.

There are some grounds for dismissal that can never be acceptable.

- Where the dismissal is 'union-related', for example, because the employee took part in trade union activities.
- Where the dismissal is on the grounds of pregnancy.
- Where the dismissal is on the grounds of redundancy and the selection procedure was unfair.
- Where the dismissal took place on the transfer of an undertaking.

Thirdly, however, even if you can show that there was an acceptable ground for dismissing an employee, an Industrial Tribunal will still have to decide whether the dismissal was, in all the circumstances, fair or unfair. This is basically a test of whether the procedure followed was fair, that is, whether there was a known disciplinary procedure which should have been followed for the dismissal to be fair.

Finally, for an employee to claim that he has been unfairly dismissed, he must present his claim to an Industrial Tribunal within three months of the effective date of the termination of the employment, or some other period considered reasonable where it is not practical to comply with that time limit.

7. YOUR ACCOUNTING AND FINANCIAL RESPONSIBILITIES

Page

What accounting records must a company keep? 73

How long must accounting records be kept? 75

Where can my company keep its accounting records? 75

Can my company keep its accounting records outside Great
    Britain? 75

Am I entitled to see my company's accounting records? 76

What if proper accounting records are not kept? 76

What accounts must be prepared? 77

Can I leave all the responsibility for the accounts with the
    Finance Director? 77

Are there any restrictions on the size of dividends my company
    can pay? 78

What happens if a dividend is excessive? 79

7. YOUR ACCOUNTING AND FINANCIAL RESPONSIBILITIES

WHAT ACCOUNTING RECORDS MUST A COMPANY KEEP?

All companies are under a duty to keep accounting records. The accounting records must be sufficient to 'show and explain the company's transactions'. Further, they must disclose the financial position of the company with reasonable accuracy *at any time* and enable the directors of the company to ensure that its statutory accounts comply with the *Companies Act 1985* in terms of their form and content. In particular, this means they should contain:

- Daily entries of receipts and payments with details of what they are for.
- A record of the company's assets and liabilities.
- Where the company deals in goods, year-end stock records and any records from which these are prepared.
- Where the company deals in goods, records of all goods bought and sold, with enough detail to identify the buyers and sellers. No such record needs to be kept in the case of retail goods.

This is not the end of the story, however, and when considering the requirements governing a company's accounting records you must take into account other requirements, particularly the VAT legislation, which is not considered in this book.

The Consultative Committee of Accounting Bodies issued a Technical Release (TR573) in March 1985 to provide guidance for directors on their main financial and accounting duties and responsibilities. As best practice it recommends that:

In addition to the statutory requirement to keep proper books of account which show an up-to-date picture of the company's financial position, the directors have an overriding responsibility to ensure that they have adequate information to enable them to discharge their duty to manage the company's business.

The Institute of Chartered Accountants in April 1970 gave additional guidance (U17), recommending that:

The directors should therefore ensure that the books and accounting records are:
(a) Adequate to meet the statutory requirements;
(b) Kept up to date;
(c) Designed so as to facilitate:

(i) Safeguarding the company's assets, and

(ii) The prompt preparation of accounting and management information, adequate for the proper control of the particular business.

The accounting and management information should be in sufficient detail to enable the directors to control, *inter alia*:

(a) Cash;
(b) Debtors and creditors;
(c) Capital expenditure;
(d) Stock and work in progress.

In addition, a plan should be prepared against which the subsequent performance of the business can be measured. Periodic management accounts will be necessary to enable actual operating results and cash position to be compared with plan. The extent and frequency of the preparation of such accounts and the level of management to which they are presented will depend on the size, scope and nature of the business.

In practice, a company's normal accounting records would include:

- Cash books.
- Sales day book.
- Sales return book.
- Purchase day book.
- Purchase returns book.
- Creditors' ledger.
- Debtors' ledger.
- Transfer journal.
- General ledger.

Company law permits these to be retained on a computer (although bear in mind Customs & Excise requirements referred to above), or in other suitable readable form. These accounting records form the basis of what is called a 'double-entry bookkeeping system'. If you are incorporating an existing business you may already be familiar with such a system. If you are setting up in business for the first time, your accountants will be able to help you decide a system appropriate for your business and help to explain how it can be operated.

Your record-keeping obligations do not finish with your accounting records, although these are very important. There are various payroll records that you must keep, for example as to statutory sick pay (see page 65). Depending on the type of information you store and the way in which you store it, you may need to comply with the *Data Protection Act 1984*. Specialised types of business may also be subject to special requirements. For example, if you are an 'investment business' you will have to comply with various record-keeping requirements so as to comply with the *Financial Services Act 1986*.

HOW LONG MUST ACCOUNTING RECORDS BE KEPT?

Company law only requires a private company to keep its accounting records for three years from the date when they are prepared and a public company for six years. However, there are a number of other considerations. For example, all companies registered for VAT must keep certain records for at least six years. A similar period is recommended for records related to tax generally, since the Inland Revenue can assess you for tax for six years after a chargeable period. You may decide that a longer period is necessary, for example, in an architects' practice the architects may be liable for professional negligence claims for many years.

In commercial terms, the view is frequently taken that all records should be destroyed as soon as possible to save storage space and therefore cost. However, modern methods of microfilming enable documents to be retained at little cost in legible form. If you are setting up in business for the first time you should discuss the period necessary for keeping your particular records with your professional advisors. If your company is established and substantial, you should consider nominating a person to be responsible for document retention so that a consistent policy is applied and maintained.

WHERE CAN MY COMPANY KEEP ITS ACCOUNTING RECORDS?

A company can keep its accounting records either at its registered office or any other place that the directors decide upon.

CAN MY COMPANY KEEP ITS ACCOUNTING RECORDS OUTSIDE GREAT BRITAIN?

Yes. However, if the company does so, 'accounts and returns' must be sent to an appropriate place in Great Britain (for example, the company's registered office) where they must be available for inspection at all times. These accounts and returns should show the company's financial position at intervals not exceeding six months.

They should also enable the directors to ensure that the company's financial statements comply with the rules on form and content set out in the *Companies Act 1985* (see page 73).

AM I ENTITLED TO SEE MY COMPANY'S ACCOUNTING RECORDS?

Yes. Although the accounting records are usually made the responsibility of one particular director (for example, the Finance Director) they must be available for inspection by the company's officers at all times.

WHAT IF PROPER ACCOUNTING RECORDS ARE NOT KEPT?

First, where a company fails to keep or preserve accounting records *every* officer of the company who is in default commits a criminal offence, *unless* he can show that he acted honestly and that the default was excusable in the circumstances in which the company's business was carried on. However, an offence will be committed where an officer of a company fails to take all reasonable steps to ensure that the company keeps these accounting records for the required period, *or* has intentionally caused any default by the company in this respect. If a person is convicted on trial or indictment he can be imprisoned for a maximum of two years and/or given an unlimited fine. On summary trial he can be imprisoned for a maximum of six months and/or given a fine of up to £2,000. A table of criminal offences is given in Appendix III.

Prosecutions are rare. However, you should remember that your company's auditors are placed under a specific duty to carry out such investigations as will enable them to form an opinion as to whether your company has kept proper accounting records and whether proper returns adequate for their audit have been received from branches not visited by them. If they cannot come to such an opinion, or their opinion has to be qualified in some way, this will be mentioned in their audit report. Although that may not sound a serious sanction, remember that it may come to the attention of the DTI, Customs & Excise and the Inland Revenue, or possibly concern your company's bankers. The consequences could then be serious.

In addition, you should remember that the extent of your responsibility for a failure by your company to comply with the company law provision in respect of company records is a factor that could later be taken into account by a court assessing whether you are 'unfit' to be a director and should, therefore, be disqualified (see page 119).

WHAT ACCOUNTS MUST BE PREPARED?

The directors of every company are responsible for the company preparing:

- A profit and loss account (or an income and expenditure account if the company does not trade for profit), in respect of each accounting reference period of the company.
- A balance sheet as at the last date of the company's financial year.
- A directors' report, for each financial year.
- Group accounts, where a company has subsidiaries at its year end.

Together with the auditor's report, these comprise a company's 'accounts' for legal purposes. This book also uses the term 'financial statements', which is a term adopted by the accounting bodies to refer to the accounts.

All companies (other than banking, insurance and some shipping companies) must prepare their accounts on the basis of standard formats set out in the *Companies Act 1985*. These standard formats are in use throughout the European Community. In addition, there are detailed requirements for the content of company accounts. The legal requirement, however, is that the profit and loss account and balance sheet must give 'a true and fair view' of the company or group's profit or loss for the financial year and its state of affairs at the end of that year. You can find detailed information about the legal requirements in *The Accounting Provisions of the Companies Act 1985*, Johnson and Patient, (Farringdon, 1985).

CAN I LEAVE ALL THE RESPONSIBILITY FOR THE ACCOUNTS WITH THE FINANCE DIRECTOR?

No. Company law places the duty to prepare a company's accounts on the directors of a company. Although much of the detailed work relating to this will (and ought) to be delegated to the Finance Director, this does not absolve other directors from their overall responsibility. As considered below (see page 119), the way in which you discharge this responsibility could affect a decision as to whether you are disqualified as a director. The directors' collective responsibility for the accounts is also indicated by the legal requirement that the accounts must be approved by the board and then *two* of the directors of the company must sign its balance sheet (and every copy of it laid before the company in a general meeting or filed with the Registrar of Companies) *on behalf of* the board.

Additionally, company law prescribes penalties where accounts or group accounts are laid before a general meeting of a company or filed with the Registrar of Companies that do not comply with the *Companies Act 1985* disclosure requirements. On trial or indictment *all* the directors are liable to an unlimited fine, or on summary trial a fine to a maximum of £2,000. It is a defence, however, if you can show that you took all reasonable steps to secure compliance with the requirements in question.

ARE THERE ANY RESTRICTIONS ON THE SIZE OF DIVIDENDS MY COMPANY CAN PAY?

Yes. The extent of the restrictions will depend upon whether your company is a private company or a public company and the rules are complex.

- Private companies
  The principles are summarised below:

  - Profits and losses must be 'accumulated' from one year to the next. So if you make a loss in one year, this must be made good by profits in another year before you can pay a dividend.
  - Only 'realised' profits can be distributed. Whether a profit is 'realised' or 'unrealised' has to be determined in accordance with generally accepted accounting principles. For example, in general, a revaluation of an asset does not give rise to a 'realised' profit.
  - In calculating your accumulated realised profit or loss you must take into account any distributions or capitalisation already made and any losses written off in a capital reduction or reorganisation.
  - The directors can then only make a distribution where it is in the company's best interests generally.

- Public companies
  The principles that apply to private companies apply equally to public companies, but in addition there are the following requirements:

  - Unrealised losses must be made good out of realised profits in so far as they exceed unrealised profits.

– Unrealised profits that have been distributed and not subsequently realised must be made good by realised profits.

There are further special provisions that relate to investment companies.

WHAT HAPPENS IF A DIVIDEND IS EXCESSIVE?

A shareholder is liable to repay a dividend to his company if he knew, or had reasonable grounds to know, that it was being paid in breach of the requirements. Furthermore, the directors may be held liable to the company if it appeared that they had paid a dividend without having sufficient realised reserves to do so.

8. SHAREHOLDERS' MEETINGS

Page

What is a shareholders' meeting? 81

Does the company need to hold regular meetings? 81

What has to be done at an annual general meeting? 81

Who is responsible for holding the annual general meeting? 82

When must an extraordinary general meeting be held? 82

How much notice should be given for a shareholders' meeting? ... 83

Where should a shareholders' meeting be held? 84

Do all the directors have to be present at a shareholders' meeting? 85

Should there be a chairman of a shareholders' meeting? 85

Can I attend a shareholders' meeting if I am not a shareholder? .. 85

How many shareholders need to attend a shareholders' meeting?. 86

What majority is needed for a resolution to be passed at a shareholders' meeting? 86

What happens after a resolution is adopted at a general meeting? 88

8. SHAREHOLDERS' MEETINGS

WHAT IS A SHAREHOLDERS' MEETING?

As noted earlier, the shareholders of a company are its owners. As a director you are responsible for the company's management and, therefore, accountable to the company's owners. At a shareholders' meeting the shareholders meet formally and may discuss and determine the company's future, taking the decisions that are, by law or by the company's Articles of Association, required of them.

DOES THE COMPANY NEED TO HOLD REGULAR MEETINGS?

There must be an 'annual general meeting' ('AGM') which must be held in each calendar year and within fifteen months of the last such meeting. Where a company is newly incorporated the first AGM must be held within eighteen months of incorporation. It would be unusual for a company to have any other regular meeting, but this is possible. Any other meeting is called an 'extraordinary general meeting' ('EGM'). This type of meeting is considered on page 82 below.

WHAT HAS TO BE DONE AT AN ANNUAL GENERAL MEETING?

This will depend on the company's Articles of Association.

Table A only requires that the retirement of a company's first directors is considered at the first AGM and that the retirement of directors by rotation is considered at each AGM.

In practice, it is also customary (and convenient) for an annual general meeting to cover the following:

- The adoption of the accounts for the most recent financial year.
- Reading the audit report on the accounts to the meeting.
- A resolution to reappoint the auditors and to pay them a fee.
- A resolution to pay the directors a fee.

Many companies will have adopted Table A prior to 1 July 1985 when the new Table A was introduced. The changes in the new Table A do not apply to existing companies, unless specifically adopted by them. If your company is subject to the old Table A, you will find that its Articles of Association distinguish between 'ordinary' business and 'special' business. 'Special' business can only be validly transacted if its general nature is summarised in the notice to the meeting. Under the new Table A an indication must be given in the notice of the meeting of all business. 'Ordinary' business under the old Table A consisted of the declaration of a dividend, consideration of the accounts, balance sheets and directors' and auditors' reports, the election of directors in place of those retiring and the appointment of auditors and the fixing of their remuneration. 'Special' business was anything else.

Your company's register of directors' interest in shares and debentures must be available for inspection or accessible at the AGM (see page 104).

If the company in question is listed on The Stock Exchange, The Stock Exchange's Yellow Book additionally requires that copies of all directors' service contracts of more than one year's duration or, where the contract is not in writing, a memorandum of its terms, must be made available for inspection at the company's registered office or share transfer office during usual business hours. They must be made available on any weekday from the date of the notice for the AGM *and* at the place of the meeting for at least fifteen minutes prior to the meeting and at the meeting itself.

WHO IS RESPONSIBLE FOR HOLDING THE ANNUAL GENERAL MEETING?

In practice, the company secretary will be delegated the responsibility of arranging the AGM. However, legally both the company and all its officers are responsible for any failure to hold an AGM. The maximum penalty on trial on indictment is an unlimited fine. On summary trial the penalty is limited to a fine of £2,000.

WHEN MUST AN EXTRAORDINARY GENERAL MEETING BE HELD?

Table A leaves it to you, as the directors of a company, to call an EGM whenever you think fit. You must, however, call an EGM in the following situations:

- Shareholders' requisition
  The directors have to call an EGM where shareholders holding at least 10% of the paid up voting share capital of the company formally require this. The formal 'requisition' must state the purpose of the meeting, be signed by those requiring the meeting and be deposited at the registered office of the company. If the

directors do not call the meeting within twenty-one days, then those who called the meeting (or holders of more than half their voting rights) may call the meeting themselves within three months. The company will then have to pay the expenses of this meeting and must deduct it from the directors' remuneration.

- Court order

Where for any reason it is impracticable for a meeting to be called or conducted in the way prescribed by a company's Articles of Association or by law, a court may order an EGM to be called, held and conducted in any manner it thinks fit.

- Serious loss of the company's capital

The directors of a public company must call an EGM if their company suffers a serious loss of capital, where its net assets fall to half or less of its called up share capital. The meeting must be called no later than twenty-eight days from the relevant date when the loss is known to a director of the company and must actually be held at a date no later than fifty-six days from that date. The purpose of the meeting is to consider whether (and if so, what) steps should be taken to deal with the situation. If no meeting is called, each director who 'knowingly and wilfully' authorises the failure to call the meeting (or subsequently permits it to continue) is liable on conviction on indictment to an unlimited fine, or on summary trial to a fine up to a maximum of £2,000.

In addition, the Articles of Association may permit shareholders to call a meeting themselves.

HOW MUCH NOTICE SHOULD BE GIVEN FOR A SHAREHOLDERS' MEETING?

The law requires twenty-one days notice to be given for an AGM unless the shareholders *all* agree to a shorter period. For other meetings fourteen days notice must be given unless the holders of 95% of the share capital agree to a shorter period. A company's Articles of Association *may* specify longer periods than these, but this is unusual.

There are certain types of resolution for which 'special notice' must be given to the company by the person proposing the notice. Special notice is notice to the company of the intention to put forward a particular resolution. It must be given no less than twenty-eight days before the meeting. However, even if a meeting is subsequently called in less than the required period, the notice is deemed to have been validly given. Otherwise the directors could frustrate the purpose of a resolution (for example, to remove a director) by calling a meeting at short notice and then arguing that any dismissal was invalid.

When the company receives a special notice it must give notice of the intended resolution to its shareholders at the same time and in the same way as it gives notice of the meeting. If that is impracticable, it must advertise the notice in a newspaper of 'appropriate circulation' (or as otherwise permitted in the company's Articles of Association) no less than twenty-one days before the meeting.

The circumstances where special notice is required include:

- To appoint or retain a director of a public company, or of its subsidiary, who has reached seventy years old.
- Where the effect of certain resolutions is to appoint a new auditor or to remove an old auditor.
- To dismiss a director.

The Courts have taken the view that 'days' mean 'clear days', and so in all the situations above you should exclude the day that a shareholder receives the notice and the day of the meeting itself in counting the number of days. For example, if you wish to hold an annual general meeting on 31 March, you must ensure that the notice is posted on 3 March. The reason for the additional two days is that Table A states that a notice will be deemed to be given at the expiration of forty-eight hours after the envelope containing it was posted. You are well advised in any event to leave ample time for the notice to be received and also to retain proof that the envelopes containing the notice were properly addressed, prepaid and posted. This is because Table A deems that such proof is *conclusive* evidence that you have given the notice.

WHERE SHOULD A SHAREHOLDERS' MEETING BE HELD?

There are no legal restrictions on where a shareholders' meeting should be held. This will be a practical question for the directors to consider. In a small private company where the directors are the only shareholders, the directors may decide to hold their meeting either at the company's place of business, or at their homes, or in the board room that many firms of accountants make available for this purpose. The possibility of holding a meeting by telephone is considered, in the context of board meetings, on page 53. One difference in relation to shareholders' meetings is that, unless the Articles of Association provide otherwise, the *quorum* for a meeting can only be constituted by shareholders attending *personally*. Although Table A makes provision for attendance by proxy or by an authorised representative of a company, there is no provision for the meeting to be held other than in person.

DO ALL THE DIRECTORS HAVE TO BE PRESENT AT A SHAREHOLDERS' MEETING?

No. In fact Table A specifically caters for the situation where there is no director present at all, in that it permits the shareholders to elect one of themselves to chair the meeting if no director arrives within fifteen minutes of the meeting being called.

At a company's AGM, particularly in the case of a large company, it is advisable for all directors to attend. Often the AGM is the only occasion when the directors of a company can be called to account for their stewardship of the company and answer questions. Frequently, a question can only be meaningfully and accurately answered by the director responsible for the particular area of the company's business. However, there may be an EGM (see page 82) held for a particular purpose where your attendance may be unnecessary. In such a situation, it is courteous to send your apologies.

SHOULD THERE BE A CHAIRMAN OF A SHAREHOLDERS' MEETING?

Yes. If the directors have elected a chairman of the board of directors (see page 54) Table A provides that he should preside as chairman of a shareholders' meeting. Where the chairman of the board is neither present, nor willing to act, within fifteen minutes of the meeting commencing, the directors present must elect one of themselves as chairman. If only one director is present, he must act as chairman if he is willing to do so. Failing this, Table A provides that the shareholders present who can vote must choose one of themselves to be chairman of the meeting.

CAN I ATTEND A SHAREHOLDERS' MEETING IF I AM NOT A SHAREHOLDER?

You are entitled as a director under Table A to attend and speak at any shareholders' meeting whether or not you are a shareholder.

Those who are neither shareholders, nor directors, are not entitled to attend, although some public companies will permit outsiders to attend, for example, members of the Press.

HOW MANY SHAREHOLDERS NEED TO
ATTEND A SHAREHOLDERS' MEETING?

Unless your company's Articles of Association provide otherwise, the *Companies Act 1985* states that there must be two shareholders present in person to constitute a meeting. The new Table A varies this by providing that personal attendance can include attendance by proxy or by an authorised representative of a company. If your company's Articles of Association are in the form of Table A and were registered prior to 22 December 1980, the *quorum* required will be *three* shareholders present in person, and proxies will not be allowed for this purpose.

You should note that if a shareholder dies his personal representative will become entitled to his shareholding. Frequently, a personal representative will not actually give notice to the company requesting to be entered on the register of members as a shareholder. Unless this is done, the personal representative is not entitled to vote and will not count towards the *quorum*. This may mean that the company will only have one shareholder and this can cause serious problems (see page 113).

If insufficient shareholders turn up, so that a *quorum* is not established, the meeting will automatically be adjourned half an hour after the time when it was due to commence. The meeting will then stand adjourned until the same time a week later at the same place (unless the directors decide on a different time and place). If the meeting was called by the shareholders in the first place, the meeting will be automatically dissolved.

If your company's Articles of Association are in the form of Table A and were registered prior to 22 December 1980, they will additionally provide that where a *quorum* is not present within half an hour at the adjourned meeting, the members present will constitute a *quorum* for that meeting.

WHAT MAJORITY IS NEEDED FOR A RESOLUTION
TO BE PASSED AT A SHAREHOLDERS' MEETING?

This will depend on the nature of the resolution. Unless the resolution falls into one of the categories below, where there are special requirements, it can be passed by a simple majority of members voting on the resolution. Such a resolution is called an 'ordinary resolution'.

Many of the more important changes that a company's shareholders are responsible for approving must be passed by a 'special resolution'.

A special resolution has to be passed by 75% of shareholders in a general meeting where twenty-one days or more notice has been given. Usually the number of votes each shareholder has will not be counted and the chairman of the meeting will simply declare the resolution carried on the strength of a show of hands. A shareholder may demand that a 'poll' is taken; if this is so, the number or proportion of votes held by shareholders will be counted. In this situation, the majority will be ascertained by counting the number of votes cast for or against the resolution.

A special resolution is required in a number of situations including the following:

- To change a company's objects.
- To alter a company's Articles of Association.
- To alter any condition in a company's Memorandum of Association that could lawfully have been in its Articles of Association instead.
- To change the company's name.
- To allow a private company to re-register as a public company or *vice-versa*.
- To re-register an unlimited company as a private limited company.
- To resolve not to appoint auditors where the company is dormant.
- To allow directors to ignore shareholders' pre-emption rights.
- To decide that any uncalled share capital should not be called up except on the company's winding up.
- To reduce the company's share capital.
- To approve the giving of financial assistance by a private company for the acquisition of its or its holding company's shares.
- To authorise the terms of a proposed contract for an off-market purchase of the company's own shares.
- To authorise the terms of a contingent purchase contract.
- To approve a payment out of capital to redeem or purchase the company's shares.
- To alter the company's Memorandum of Association to render the directors', managers' or any managing director's liability un-limited.
- To approve the assignment by a director or manager of his office to another person.
- To resolve that the company be wound up.
- To approve the acceptance by a liquidator in a members' voluntary winding up (see page 136) of shares in another company in exchange for the assets of the company.

Certain important company resolutions need to be passed with speed. In this event ordinary notice will suffice, but the same majority of votes is required as for a special resolution.

An extraordinary resolution is required in the following circumstances:

- Where class rights are to be varied.
- To put the company into a voluntary winding up.
- To give the liquidator in a members' voluntary winding up various powers to deal with creditors.

WHAT HAPPENS AFTER A RESOLUTION IS ADOPTED AT A GENERAL MEETING?

Copies of most resolutions have to be forwarded to the Registrar of Companies and recorded by him within fifteen days after the resolution is passed. A copy of the resolution then has to be embodied in, or annexed to, every copy of the company's articles issued after the resolution. The resolutions to which these rules apply, are as follows:

- Special resolutions.
- Extraordinary resolutions.
- Resolutions that would have been special resolutions or extra-ordinary resolutions if they had not otherwise been agreed by all of the members of the company.
- Resolutions that have been agreed to by all the members of a particular class of shareholders.
- A resolution passed to change the company's name on the direction of the Secretary of State.
- A resolution to revoke or renew an authority to the directors to allot shares or securities.
- A resolution passed by a company to alter its memorandum on ceasing to be a public company, following an acquistion of its own shares.
- A resolution conferring, varying, revoking or renewing an authority for the company to purchase its own shares in the market.
- A resolution for a voluntary winding up of the company.

If the company fails to comply with these requirements every officer who is in default is liable to a fine on summary conviction of £400 and a daily default fine of £40.

9. YOUR REMUNERATION AS A DIRECTOR

Page

How will my remuneration as a director be determined? 90

Can the shareholders find out how much I am paid? 91

Can I borrow money from my company? 92

Can I get around these borrowing restrictions by setting up a subsidiary company to make me the loan? 93

Can I get a third party to lend me the money with my company merely guaranteeing the loan? 93

I suppose then that I am not allowed to get the company to make a loan to a connected person? 94

Are there any other restrictions on public companies? 94

After all that, what is a 'loan' anyway? 94

Could this definition cover an expense advance? 95

What are 'quasi-loans' and how do they affect me? 96

What are 'credit transactions' and how do they affect me? 96

In all these situations can't I just take out the loan, say from my bank, and then get the company to take it over? 97

What happens if I break one of these rules about loans, quasi-loans and credit transactions? 98

Are there any rules regarding other transactions I might enter into? 98

How will anyone find out about it? 99

What details will have to be disclosed? 99

When can I get out of having to disclose these transactions? 100

What happens if details of these transactions are omitted from my company's financial statements? 101

9. YOUR REMUNERATION AS A DIRECTOR

HOW WILL MY REMUNERATION AS A DIRECTOR BE DETERMINED?

In many respects this is a practical question and the legal framework is of little relevance. The circumstances of companies vary to such a great extent that it is difficult to lay down any general principles. For example, if you are setting up your own business in the form of a company, then, subject to taxation and the business' requirements, you will want to get as much money out of the company as you can. If you and your spouse are the only shareholders as well, then this will not be difficult. However, the position of directors of substantial listed companies may be different. One example is the controversy which arose over the remuneration package proposed for Sir Ralph Halpern of The Burton Group PLC and the modification of this following institutional shareholders' pressure.

Table A entitles a director to reimbursement of his expenses only. Other remuneration must be determined by the company's share-holders by ordinary resolution in a general meeting. Where a director has no executive function he is entirely dependent on the shareholders for his remuneration. This applies, for example, where a director only attends board meetings and signs company documents. Where, however, a director supplies additional services (for example, of an executive nature) to his company, then in legal terms the director is entitled to a reasonable payment for these services, known as *quantum meruit*. Furthermore, a director may be an employee of the company as well, in that event he will be entitled to the remuneration agreed in his contract of service.

In practice, a director in considering his remuneration will not purely be concerned with the salary receivable, but also with the entire package.

The Institute of Directors in its *Guide to Boardroom Practice – The Remuneration of Executive Directors* considers the machinery for approving executive remuneration. It says:

> The cardinal principle for approving the remuneration of executive directors is that some objective party should play a part if the remuneration is paid in circumstances in which conflicts of interest could arise.

In particular, and this applies especially to listed companies, the Guide considers that while it is possible and desirable for the general meeting of shareholders to have overall control of directors' remuneration, *complex* executive remuneration packages are wholly inappropriate subjects for such a body to consider. Accordingly, it recommends the establishment of a board committee (a 'remuneration committee') made up of the chairman and the non-executive directors. This should consider the amount of, and the manner of, payment of executive remuneration. Several well known public companies, such as The BOC Group plc and Tate & Lyle plc, have remuneration committees.

CAN THE SHAREHOLDERS FIND OUT HOW MUCH I AM PAID?

Possibly. Depending upon your position and your company's circumstances, your company's shareholders and anyone else who obtains a copy of your company's financial statements may be able to find out some details of your remuneration.

You are under a legal duty to give your company information about your remuneration so that the information can be disclosed in its financial statements. This applies even where you have been a director of a company in any of the previous five years. If you fail to do so, you are liable to be fined. On trial on indictment the fine is unlimited. On summary trial it is limited to a maximum of £2,000.

The remuneration you disclose should include all amounts you are paid for being a director of the company, whether you are paid by it, by a subsidiary or by some third party. So, if you were to set up a company to receive the remuneration on your behalf, that would need to be disclosed as well. Nor can you avoid disclosure by getting your company to arrange for your appointment as a nominee director of a totally independent company. Your remuneration in respect of that appointment would need to be disclosed. However, if you are appointed director mid-way through the year, the financial statements need only show your remuneration as director and *not* your salary as an employee before becoming a director.

The *Companies Act 1985* does *not*, however, require your company's financial statements to show the remuneration you have disclosed to the company individually. All that is required is that the notes to your company's profit and loss account show the total amount of *all* the directors' emoluments as directors. The note must split the amounts received between remuneration as directors and otherwise (for example, any professional fees you bill to your company). The directors' emoluments, for this purpose, include not only their salaries, but also any expense allowance, pension scheme contributions and the estimated money value of any benefits in kind. The total figure given should not only be in respect of your own company, but also in respect of your services as director *or* manager of both the company and any of its subsidiaries.

However, one small loophole does exist in the legislation. You do not need to disclose a pension scheme contribution payment made in respect of two or more persons, if the amount paid in respect of each of them cannot be ascertained separately. For example, if your company was to make either a payment of a lump sum to a pension scheme or a premium to an insurance company for a pension scheme, and the calculation in respect of each director cannot be separately identified, *no* amount has to be disclosed as directors' emoluments in respect of those pension contributions.

If your company is *not* part of a group of companies and the total directors' emoluments shown in the financial statements are £60,000 or less, the requirements above are all you need satisfy. However, other companies (except those that are entitled to file modified accounts for a small company) must include the following additional information:

- The bands into which the emoluments of *all* directors fall must be disclosed. These bands are £0 to £5,000, £5,001 to £10,000 and so on.
- The chairman's emoluments must be separately disclosed. Where there has been more than one chairman, the information must be disclosed for the period served by each Chairman. In this context the 'chairman' will be the person elected to chair directors' meetings.
- The highest paid director's emoluments must be separately disclosed, unless he was the chairman.
- Where directors have waived their rights to emoluments, the number of directors and amount of emoluments waived must be disclosed.

In all these cases emoluments do *not* include pension contributions. None of this disclosure is required in respect of directors who worked wholly or mainly outside the U.K.

So, in practice, unless your company is obliged to disclose your emoluments where you are chairman or the highest paid director, a shareholder will not be able to find out from your company's financial statements the exact amount of your remuneration.

CAN I BORROW MONEY FROM MY COMPANY?

No. A company (whether public or private) may not make a loan to a director, unless the total of such transactions does not exceed £2,500. Any loans to a director's 'connected persons' have to be taken into account in determining whether he is within this limit.

A 'connected person' is a person whom the law regards as capable of being influenced by a director. The more important examples of a 'connected person' are:

- Your wife or husband.
- Your children (even if illegitimate), or step-children until they reach eighteen years of age.
- A company with which you are 'associated'. Broadly speaking you are associated with a company if you and your other connected persons either are interested in at least 20% of the equity share capital, or are able to exercise or control at least 20% of the voting power at any general meeting.
- Any person who is a trustee where the beneficiaries of the trust include you or your connected persons as defined above, or where the trustees have a power under the trust to exercise it for the connected persons' benefit.
- Any person who is your partner or a partner of your connected persons.

However, none of these persons above are 'connected persons' if they are also directors of the company.

The definition of 'connected person' is important and will be referred to on other occasions in this book. Decision tables to enable you to see whether loans and other transactions are legal are given in Appendix IV.

CAN I GET AROUND THESE BORROWING RESTRICTIONS BY SETTING UP A SUBSIDIARY COMPANY TO MAKE ME THE LOAN?

No. A company may not make a loan to the directors of its holding company unless it and similar loans do not exceed £2,500. Don't forget though that, subject to what is said below, a holding company *is* allowed to make loans to a director of its subsidiary, and that a subsidiary may make a loan to a director of a fellow subsidiary.

CAN I GET A THIRD PARTY TO LEND ME THE MONEY WITH MY COMPANY MERELY GUARANTEEING THE LOAN?

No. A company may not enter into any guarantee or indemnity, or provide any security, in connection with a loan a third party makes to either a director of a company, or a director of its holding company.

I SUPPOSE THEN THAT I AM NOT ALLOWED TO GET
THE COMPANY TO MAKE A LOAN TO A 'CONNECTED PERSON'?

Surprisingly, after what has been said above, this may be possible. An important distinction that has to be made is whether you are a director of what is termed a 'relevant' or a 'non-relevant' company. A 'relevant' company is either a public company, or a company that belongs to a group which contains a public company. All other companies are 'non-relevant' companies. For simplicity, in this chapter 'relevant' companies are referred to as 'public' companies and 'non-relevant' companies are referred to as 'private' companies. Do remember however, that the wider definition is the correct one.

A private company may make a loan to a director's connected person of any amount, provided that it has power to do so in its Memorandum and Articles of Association. Such a loan is unlawful, however, if a public company makes it, regardless of its size. If your company is contemplating making such a loan, you should also bear in mind your fiduciary duties as a director (see page 44).

ARE THERE ANY OTHER RESTRICTIONS ON PUBLIC COMPANIES?

Yes. A public company is, in addition, not allowed to enter into any guarantee, or provide any security, in connection with a third party making a loan to a director or a director's connected person. On the other hand, a public company is not prohibited from making a loan or quasi-loan (or entering into a guarantee, etc) to another group company. This applies even where the director of the public company is associated (see page 93) with that other group company.

Furthermore, the exception in respect of small loans (see page 93) does not apply to loans that public companies make to a director's connected person. Nor does it apply to guarantees, etc, that such companies provide to directors or their connected persons.

AFTER ALL THAT, WHAT IS A LOAN, ANYWAY?

The expression 'loan' is not defined in the *Companies Act 1985*. However, it was interpreted in a case brought under the *Companies Act 1948*, where it was held that the dictionary definition of a 'loan' as a 'sum of money lent for a time to be returned in money or money's worth' applied. [*Champagne Perrier–Jouet S.A. v. H. H. Finch Ltd.* [1982] 1 WLR 1359.]

COULD THIS DEFINITION COVER AN EXPENSE ADVANCE?

Quite possibly. Usually expense advances will be outside the definition above because they are not intended to be repaid, but to be used for the benefit of the company. However, circumstances may arise where the amount advanced is clearly excessive or remains unspent for an unduly long time. It may be that such an expense advance could be construed as a loan if it were contemplated that the amount should be repaid at some future time, whilst, in the meantime, the director derived a personal benefit from holding the money.

The *Companies Act 1985* does, however, permit companies to give you funds, as a director, to enable you to perform properly your duties as an officer of the company. A company may do this by way of loan, quasi-loan (see page 96) or credit transaction (see page 96) or any other similar arrangement. This exemption applies, however, only if one of the following two conditions is satisfied:

- The transaction has been approved in advance by the company in general meeting. At that general meeting, the purpose of the expenditure, the amount of the funds to be provided, and the extent of the company's liability under the transaction must all be made known.
- It is a condition of the transaction that, if the company does not subsequently approve the transaction at or before the next annual general meeting, the director will discharge, within six months, the liability that arises under the transaction.

A public company can only enter into such a transaction if the total of such transactions does not exceed £10,000. There is no upper limit on transactions of this type in the case of private companies.

The most common form of transaction of this nature is a bridging loan a company gives to a director who changes location within the company and so needs to move house.

Note, however, that these provisions do not restrict normal sized advances that a company makes to a director for business expenditure. Consequently, these types of transaction are permitted without first needing to be approved in general meeting. This is because the funds the company provides to the director in this way are not lent to him.

WHAT ARE 'QUASI-LOANS' AND HOW DO THEY AFFECT ME?

If you are a director of a private company (see page 94), you will not be affected by the rules regarding quasi-loans.

A 'quasi-loan' is an arrangement under which your company meets some of your financial obligations on the understanding that you will reimburse the company later.

The value of a quasi-loan is the amount, or maximum amount, that the person receiving it is liable to reimburse.

A common example of a quasi-loan arises where a director uses a company credit card to buy personal goods, and he does so on the understanding that the company will settle the liability and he will reimburse the company at a later date. Another example, is the type of arrangement whereby companies in a group pay for goods and services for the personal use of a director of the holding company, on the basis that he will reimburse those companies at a later date.

A private company (see page 94) may make a quasi-loan of any amount to either the company's directors or its holding company's directors, or to their connected persons. They may also guarantee or provide security in respect of a quasi-loan to such a person.

A public company (see page 94) may make a quasi-loan to a director (but not to his connected persons) provided that the total amount of quasi-loans outstanding in favour of that director does not exceed £1,000, and provided also that he is required to repay each quasi-loan within two months. The total amount of quasi-loans will include such loans made by the company or by any of its subsidiaries to the director concerned, or, if the director is also a director of the company's holding company, by any fellow subsidiary.

Public companies are further restricted in that they may not enter into a guarantee or provide security for a quasi-loan a third party makes to either a director or his connected persons. However, where such a company is a member of a group, it is not prohibited either from making a quasi-loan to another member of that group or from entering into a guarantee or providing security for any such quasi-loan, by reason only that a director of one of the group companies is associated (see page 93) with another group company.

WHAT ARE 'CREDIT TRANSACTIONS' AND HOW DO THEY AFFECT ME?

If you are a director of a private company, you will not be affected by the rules regarding credit transactions.

A 'credit transaction' is any transaction where a creditor:

- Supplies any goods or any land under either a hire purchase agreement, or a conditional sale agreement.
- Leases any land or hires any goods in return for periodic payments.
- Disposes of land, or supplies goods or services, on the understanding that the payment (whatever form it takes) is to be deferred.

Note that 'services' has a very wide meaning here. It includes anything other than goods or land.

A public company can enter into credit transactions with a director provided that the total amount of such transactions does not exceed £5,000. But a public company is prohibited from entering into a credit transaction for the benefit of its directors, its holding company's directors or of a relative of a director in excess of these amounts.

The value of this type of transaction is the price that could usually be obtained for the goods, land or services that the transaction relates to if they had been supplied in the ordinary course of the company's business and on the same terms (apart from price). If the value of the transaction cannot be ascertained, then it will be assumed to be in excess of £50,000. This means that the procedures for a 'substantial property transaction' will need to be followed (see page 99).

Alternatively, a public company can in certain circumstances enter into credit transactions for *any* amount. It can do so where the value and the terms that the company offers the credit transaction to the director on are no more favourable than the value and the terms the company would have offered to someone of similar financial standing, but who is unconnected with the company.

IN ALL THESE SITUATIONS, CAN'T I JUST TAKE OUT THE LOAN, SAY FROM MY BANK, AND THEN GET THE COMPANY TO TAKE IT OVER?

No. Neither private nor public companies can arrange to have assigned to them, or to assume responsibility for, any rights, or obligations or liabilities under loans, or quasi-loans or credit transactions (or any guarantee or security in respect of these), where the transaction concerned would have been unlawful for the company to enter into. Various ways of indirectly achieving this result are also prohibited.

An example of an 'assignment' is where you get a bank loan and subsequently your company purchases the bank's rights under the loan.

An example of an 'assumption of liabilities' would occur if your father was to guarantee a bank loan to you and subsequently your company was to arrange with your father and the bank for your father to be released from the guarantee and for the company to assume the liability on it.

WHAT HAPPENS IF I BREAK ONE OF THESE RULES ABOUT LOANS, QUASI-LOANS AND CREDIT TRANSACTIONS?

The company can choose to treat the transaction as 'void' unless one of the following applies:

- It is no longer possible for the cash or property involved to be restored to the company.
- A third party has in good faith given value to acquire rights which would be affected.

Furthermore, you will be liable to account to the company for any gain you may have made as a result and to indemnify the company for any loss or damage it may suffer. However, provided that you can show that you have taken all reasonable steps to ensure that the transaction did not break the law, you will not have to account to, or indemnify, the company for a transaction where it was for a person connected with you. Furthermore, you can avoid liability if you can show that you did not know of the circumstances amounting to the contravention at the time your company entered into the transaction.

The position is far more serious if you are a director of a public company. In that situation, both the company and any directors, who, with knowledge or with reasonable cause to know of the contravention, authorised or permitted it, are guilty of a criminal offence and are liable on conviction to imprisonment or to a fine or both. The same applies to any other person who knew or had reasonable cause to know about the transaction and who procured it. Note, however, that the director's state of mind will be relevant to a court deciding whether an offence has been committed.

ARE THERE ANY RULES REGARDING OTHER TRANSACTIONS I MIGHT ENTER INTO?

Yes. Certain transactions your company or a subsidiary enters into may require to be disclosed in the financial statements if you have a 'material' interest in them. The expression material has not yet been interpreted in case law. However, Counsel has advised that material is likely to refer to whether the transaction would be of interest or relevance either to the shareholders or to the other users of the financial statements.

In addition, where you either acquire a 'non-cash asset' from your company or its holding company, or dispose of a 'non-cash asset' to your company or its holding company, there are certain requirements that you will have to comply with. These transactions are known as 'substantial property transactions'. A 'non-cash asset' in this context means any property, or any interest in property other than cash. Shareholders approval is normally required for such transactions, unless their value at the time of the arrangement is less than £1,000 (or, if value is greater than £1,000, it is less that the lower of £50,000 and 10% of the company's net assets).

HOW WILL ANYONE FIND OUT ABOUT IT?

Broadly speaking all the transactions considered above that were unlawful must be disclosed in your company's financial statements as must many lawful ones. In addition, the financial statements must disclose:

- Any agreement by your company or any of its subsidiaries to enter into such transactions for a director or connected person.
- Any other transaction or arrangement with the company or a subsidiary of it where a person who at any time during the financial year was a director of the company or its holding company has, directly or indirectly, a material interest. This also applies where a director's connected person has an interest in such a transaction.

WHAT DETAILS WILL HAVE TO BE DISCLOSED?

The following details must be disclosed in your company's financial statements about the transactions discussed above:

- The transaction's principal terms or the nature of the interest.
- A statement that the transaction either was made during the financial year or existed during that period.
- The director's name (as well as that of any connected person, if appropriate).
- The following details of any loan arrangement:

- The amount of the principal and interest both at the beginning and end of the financial year.
- The maximum amount of the liability during that period.
- The amount of any unpaid interest.

- The amount of any provision against non-payment.
- Similar details of any guarantee or security arrangement.
- The value of any transaction, or of any transaction that any other agreement relates to. For example, the disclosure is required of:

  - The amount to be reimbursed where a company buys goods on behalf of a director, or the maximum amount to be reimbursed in respect of quasi-loans (see page 96).
  - The arm's length value of any goods and services purchased in credit transactions (see page 96).

WHEN CAN I GET OUT OF HAVING TO DISCLOSE THESE TRANSACTIONS?

- In the case of your service contract, if you are a director of a listed company, you will have to disclose various details of your service contract anyway under the requirements of The Stock Exchange's Yellow Book (see page 47).
- Where the transaction is between two companies, and your interest arises only because you are also a director of the other company. The point of this is to exclude details of many general trading transactions within a group of companies.
- Somewhat obviously, where the transaction was not entered into during the period in question and did not exist during that period.
- Where the transaction is a credit transaction, or a related guarantee or assignment and the total of such transactions outstanding at any time during the relevant accounting period did not exceed £5,000.
- Where in the board's opinion, a transaction that the director has an interest in (other than a loan, quasi-loan or credit transaction) where that interest is not 'material'. For this purpose, the director with an interest in the transaction is not counted as part of the board when they vote on whether the transaction is material. Note, however, that the board's opinion must be formed in good faith.
- Where a 'material' transaction is entered into in the ordinary course of business and at arm's length.
- Where a 'material' transaction would be disclosable because you have a material interest in it, but where that interest does not

amount to any more than £1,000 in total or, if it does, does not exceed the lower of £5,000 or 1% of your company's net assets.

- Where the transaction is disclosable because you have a material interest in it, but only because you are 'associated' with your company (see page 93). No disclosure is required where your company is a member of a group and either:

  - Your company is a wholly-owned subsidiary.
  - No other group company was party to the transaction.

  The result is that the exemption is available only if minority interests are not affected.

WHAT HAPPENS IF DETAILS OF THESE TRANSACTIONS ARE OMITTED FROM MY COMPANY'S FINANCIAL STATEMENTS?

It is an offence for *any* financial statements that do not include the relevant information about transactions to be laid before a general meeting or filed with the Registrar of Companies if they do not comply with the *Companies Act 1985*. On trial on indictment, a director is liable to an unlimited fine or on summary trial to a £2,000 fine. The only defence you will have as a director is where you can *prove* that you took all reasonable steps to secure that the relevant requirements in respect of these transactions were complied with. Hence the importance of registering any protest you may have at a board meeting and having this recorded (see page 58).

Furthermore, if these disclosure requirements are not complied with, your company's auditors will have to include in their report (so far as they are reasonably able to) a statement giving the details that are omitted. The auditors are not, however, required actually to draw attention to an unlawful transaction by explicitly stating that it is unlawful or that it contravenes the *Companies Act 1985*.

10. YOUR SHAREHOLDING

Page

Can I own shares in my company?...................................... 103

Can I buy and sell shares in my company? 103

Do I have to notify my company if I buy or sell shares in it? 103

What about shares I already own when I am made a director? 103

What 'interests' in shares must I notify?.............................. 104

What if I don't notify my company?.................................... 104

With such a wide definition of 'interests' I might not even know
    that I needed to notify an interest. Could I still be convicted? .. 104

Will anyone be able to find out that I have bought or sold shares
    in my company? 104

What is insider dealing? 105

What is 'unpublished price-sensitive information'? 106

Who do the rules apply to? 106

When would a person commit an offence? 107

What are the penalties? 107

10. YOUR SHAREHOLDING

CAN I OWN SHARES IN MY COMPANY?

Yes. Directors of both private and public companies may own shares in their companies. In fact the Institute of Directors in its booklet *Guidelines for Directors* (1978) says 'in general it is desirable that directors should have a personal stake in the success or failure of their business'.

CAN I BUY AND SELL SHARES IN MY COMPANY?

As stated above, it is desirable for directors to acquire shares in their company. Legally, it is permissible for directors both to buy and sell shares in their companies. However, the purpose of directors acquiring shares in their companies is to take a personal stake in the success or failure of the business. In general, therefore, it must be undesirable for the directors to be seen to dispose of part or whole of their stake. This is even more undesirable if directors carry out such dealings with regularity so that they could be considered to be dealing in their company's shares on a short term basis. In part, this is undesirable because directors must also be assumed to have additional knowledge to that available to ordinary shareholders. Because of this, The Stock Exchange restricts such dealings by directors of public companies traded on one of its markets (see page 105).

DO I HAVE TO NOTIFY MY COMPANY IF I BUY OR SELL SHARES IN IT?

Yes. As a director (or shadow director) you must notify your company in writing of any alteration in the nature or extent of your interest in the shares (or debentures) of your company or any other group companies within five days. In calculating the five days notice you should ignore Saturdays, Sundays and bank holidays. What constitutes an interest is very widely defined by the law and covers far more than simply buying and selling shares (see below).

WHAT ABOUT SHARES I ALREADY OWN WHEN I AM MADE A DIRECTOR?

If you hold an interest in the shares (or debentures) of any company when you are made a director (or become a shadow director) of a company within the same group of companies, you must notify your company in writing of the interest within five days of your appointment.

WHAT 'INTERESTS' IN SHARES MUST I NOTIFY?

Firstly you must notify 'interests' whether they are yours, or your spouse's or your infant children's. In general terms, most interests are notifiable, for example, if you are a beneficiary under a trust. There are some exclusions, however, such as:

- Options to purchase shares.
- An interest in the shares of a subsidiary where you are also a director of its holding company. However, notification must be given to the holding company instead.

This is a complex area. If you think that you may have an interest of any sort in the shares of your company, you should take professional advice on whether you should notify it.

WHAT IF I DON'T NOTIFY MY COMPANY?

If you fail to notify your company of the matters above, you commit an offence and are liable on trial on indictment to be imprisoned for a maximum of two years and/or given an unlimited fine. On summary trial you can be imprisoned for a maximum of six months and/or given a fine limited to £2,000. An offence is also committed if you make a false statement in giving your notification.

WITH SUCH A WIDE DEFINITION OF 'INTEREST' I MIGHT NOT EVEN KNOW THAT I NEEDED TO NOTIFY AN INTEREST. COULD I STILL BE CONVICTED?

No. Your obligation to notify arises when you know that you have a notifiable interest *or* when you learn of the existence of the facts that cause an interest to be notifiable.

WILL ANYONE BE ABLE TO FIND OUT THAT I HAVE BOUGHT OR SOLD SHARES IN MY COMPANY?

Yes. All companies must maintain a register of directors' interests in shares and debentures. When your company receives your notification of an interest in it, it must record this in the register within three days (again this time limit excludes Saturdays, Sundays and bank holidays). This register is open for inspection by both shareholders in your company *and* members of the public. It must be kept either at your company's registered office or where your company's register of members is kept. It must be open for inspection for at least two hours a day during business hours. It must also be available for inspection at and be accessible at your company's AGM.

The interests in shares or debentures that are notified to your company under these rules must also be disclosed in your company's financial statements, either in the Directors' Report or in the notes to the financial statements.

Furthermore, where you are a director of a Stock Exchange listed company your company must notify The Stock Exchange Company Announcements Office of the interest by the end of the following day. In addition, more detailed disclosure of your interest will be required in the company's financial statements.

WHAT IS INSIDER DEALING?

Insider dealing has been defined as 'the conscious exploitation of confidential information to make a profit or avoid a loss by dealing in securities at a price which would have been materially altered by the publication of that information'. The confidence of the users of any market is vitally important for its success and this is no less the position with The Stock Exchange. Prices of securities should reflect their market value undistorted by any special knowledge of one party dealing in them. The sanctions against insider dealing are mainly criminal and it may be difficult for a person who has suffered loss to recover any compensation for it. The offences are laid down in the *Company Securities (Insider Dealing) Act 1985*.

The law is concerned only with dealings in securities that are traded on The Stock Exchange or on the over-the-counter market. Do not assume, however, that because you are a director of a private company, whose shares cannot be traded, that you need not be aware of these rules. The rules not only apply to directors, but can apply to any individual. For example, the rules may apply to you if your company has a business relationship with a company in whose shares you wish to deal.

There are a variety of ways in which an offence can be committed. These can be divided into three headings:

- Dealing as an insider.
- Counselling or procuring insider dealing.

- Communicating inside information.

There are two important concepts to grasp in understanding your responsibilities. These are the terms 'unpublished price sensitive information' and 'connected persons' (see below).

WHAT IS 'UNPUBLISHED PRICE SENSITIVE INFORMATION'?

This is information of a specific nature relating to, or of concern to, a company, that is not generally known to those persons who are accustomed or would be likely to deal in that company's securities. But this information would, if it were generally known, be likely to materially affect the price of that company's securities.

The value of such information in the case of a Stock Exchange listed company is usually short-lived, because such a company must in any event notify the Company Announcements Office of The Stock Exchange of any information that is necessary for shareholders and the public to appraise the company's position and to avoid a false market in its securities being created.

In the rest of this chapter 'unpublished price sensitive information' is referred to as 'inside information'.

WHO DO THE RULES APPLY TO?

The rules will apply to you if you are 'connected' with the company whose securities are in question. You will be connected with a company if you are:

- A director of it.
- An officer or employee of the company with access to inside information that you ought to keep confidential.
- You, your employer, or the company that you are a director of have a professional or business relationship with the company that gives you access to inside information that you ought to keep confidential.
- Connected with a subsidiary, fellow subsidiary or the holding company of the company in question.

The rules will also apply to you if you are what is called a 'tippee'. You will be a 'tippee' if you get inside information, and know that it is inside information, from someone who in the previous six months has been connected with the company in question, and obtained the inside information there which he ought to have treated as confidential.

The rules will *not* apply to you if you fall into one of a number of categories. The most important of these categories is that you only act, knowing that you possess inside information, without a view to making a profit or avoiding a loss. For example, the rules would not apply if you were to sell your shares only to meet an urgent financial problem.

WHEN WOULD A PERSON COMMIT AN OFFENCE?

First, a person commits an offence if he deals in a company's securities, either for himself or on behalf of someone else, if he knows that he has been connected with that company and has inside information on its securities. This would only apply, however, if it would have been reasonable to have expected him not to disclose that information except in the course of his duties.

Secondly, a person commits an offence if he passes inside information to anybody he knew (or had reasonable cause to believe) would use it to deal in those securities.

Thirdly, a person commits an offence if he passes inside information to anybody he knows (or has reasonable cause to believe) would use it to counsel or procure other people to deal in those securities.

Fourthly, a person commits an offence if he is a 'tippee' and deals in a company's securities knowing that he has inside information. This also applies to prevent a tippee from dealing in the securities of any other company where the inside information relates to any transaction (even one that is only at the proposal stage) of the company.

WHAT ARE THE PENALTIES?

If a person is tried on indictment he could be imprisoned for up to two years and/or given an unlimited fine. On summary trial he could be imprisoned for up to six months and/or given a fine of up to £2,000. However, a prosecution can only be brought by the Secretary of State for Trade and Industry or the Director of Public Prosecutions.

The transaction that a person has entered into in breach of the rules cannot be challenged and will stand, however.

11. CEASING TO BE A DIRECTOR

Page

How long can I remain a director?..................................... 109

When should I resign from being a director? 109

How do I resign? 109

How can I retire from being a director?.............................. 110

I've seen references in financial statements to 'directors retiring
    by rotation'. What does this mean? 110

Can I be dismissed from being a director? 110

Is there anything I can do to protect myself?....................... 111

Is it only the company that can dismiss me or can the board? 111

Am I entitled to compensation if I am dismissed? 111

Who can find out what compensation I get? 112

My company has two directors. We are the only shareholders.
    What happens if the other dies? 113

11. CEASING TO BE A DIRECTOR

HOW LONG CAN I REMAIN A DIRECTOR?

You can be a director for as long as your company wants you to be. As stated above (see page 33) your service contract cannot exceed five years without being approved by the members in general meeting. Even with a service contract you can be dismissed at any time (see page 110). The only legal restriction on how long you can remain a director is where you are aged over seventy (see page 24).

WHEN SHOULD I RESIGN FROM BEING A DIRECTOR?

Obviously there may be personal circumstances that will cause you to resign, such as being offered more money elsewhere, or a better job. There may be occasions when you consider resigning on a point of principle. If you do this solely as a lever in negotiations, however, you may be disappointed. Only too often has a director offered his resignation to be mortified by the chairman's brisk acceptance of it. There can be circumstances though where resignation is the best course of action open to you. For example, you may believe that your company is incurring credit whilst insolvent and fear being held liable for fraudulent or wrongful trading, and consequent disqualification as a director (see page 131). In this situation, the primary defence is for you to prove that you took every step to minimise the loss to the company's creditors. Your resignation, whilst not discharging you from responsibility, may give the Court reason to believe that you fulfilled your duties properly.

HOW DO I RESIGN?

You can resign as a director from the board at any time. Table A is representative of most Articles of Association in providing that you must give notice to the company, although it does not specify what period that notice should be for. Prior to 1 July 1985, Table A used to require *written* notice of resignation and most companies' Articles of Association will follow this, because changes in Table A do not automatically affect existing companies. Despite the requirement of writing, if you resign orally at a general meeting of the company it will be effective if the company accepts it.

On a director's resignation the company must complete Form 288 (Notice of change of directors or secretaries or in their particulars) and file it with the Registrar of Companies.

HOW CAN I RETIRE FROM BEING A DIRECTOR?

Simply by following the procedure for resignation above.

I'VE SEEN REFERENCES IN FINANCIAL STATEMENTS TO 'DIRECTORS RETIRING BY ROTATION'. WHAT DOES THIS MEAN?

Table A requires all directors to retire at the company's first AGM and, further, for one third of the directors who are subject to retirement by rotation to retire at subsequent AGMs. The original purpose of this provision was to avoid boards of directors becoming self-perpetuating and to ensure that they are regularly accountable to their shareholders. Directors should retire in the order determined by their length of service. Table A provides that the managing director and any executive director of a company are not subject to retirement by rotation. However, there is no bar to a director who has retired by rotation being proposed for re-appointment straightaway.

These provisions in Table A are frequently an inconvenience and can easily be overlooked. Many companies amend their Articles of Association to remove them.

CAN I BE DISMISSED FROM BEING A DIRECTOR?

Yes. Your company's shareholders can remove you at any time before the end of your period of office. This is regardless of anything to the contrary that there may be in the Articles of Association or your service contract. To propose such a resolution, a shareholder must give special notice. Your company is obliged to send you a copy of this proposed resolution, because you are entitled to speak at the meeting where the resolution is considered, whether or not you are a shareholder. In addition, you are entitled to make written representations of reasonable length, that the company must send to every shareholder who is sent notice of the meeting. You are entitled to require these to be read out at the meeting if your company receives them too late for them to be sent out to the shareholders.

IS THERE ANYTHING I CAN DO TO PROTECT MYSELF?

Yes. You can ask the shareholders to put what is called a 'Bushell v. Faith' clause in the company's Articles of Association. This can only be achieved in limited circumstances, and in particular, where you are not only a director but a shareholder as well. It involves the Articles of Association being amended to give your shareholding weighted voting rights on a resolution to remove you as a director. In the case which gave rise to this clause, a company's 300 shares were held equally by three persons of whom two were also directors. The company's Articles of Association weighted shareholders' voting rights from one per share to three per share when a resolution was put to a general meeting for the removal of the director holding those shares. The House of Lords upheld the validity of the clause.

This would not be appropriate in a public company, in particular, because The Stock Exchange would refuse a listing to a company that had such a clause in its Articles of Association.

IS IT ONLY THE COMPANY THAT
CAN DISMISS ME OR CAN THE BOARD?

The board cannot dismiss you unless the Articles of Association of your company permit this. Table A does not give the board such a power. It is, however, a common provision in the Articles of Association of public companies, because it enables disputes to be settled with relatively little publicity.

AM I ENTITLED TO COMPENSATION IF I AM DISMISSED?

This will depend on the manner of your dismissal and the terms of your service contract. If you are dismissed in breach of contract (for example, before your service contract is due to expire) you may be entitled to sue your company for damages as compensation. If your company had included in your service contract a clause entitling you to compensation on dismissal, then you will be entitled to that compensation. In any other situation where it is proposed to pay you compensation on dismissal, the payment will be unlawful unless particulars of the proposed payment (including its amount) are disclosed to the members of the company. The proposal has also to be approved by the company's shareholders at a general meeting. This also applies where such a payment is proposed as consideration for, or in connection with, your retirement from office.

There are three situations where you will not be entitled to any compensation for dismissal. These are:

- Where you resign or retire, except possibly where the circumstances are such that your company can be regarded as being in breach of your service contract to such an extent that what happened is in reality your dismissal. An extreme example of this would occur if your company was to prevent you from functioning as a director, for example, by excluding you from board meetings.
- Where you yourself are in fundamental breach of your service contract. For example, if you were to commit a fraud or refuse to carry out your duties, you could be dismissed on the spot.
- In certain circumstances, where your company gives you proper notice in accordance with your service contract.

Where you are also an employee of your company (see page 33), as you usually will be if you are an executive director, you will also have the statutory rights available to any employee who is unfairly dismissed, under the *Employment Protection (Consolidation) Act 1978*. Frequently, however, the statutory compensation available will not be important because of the monetary limits on what is payable. The statutory rights should not be ignored, however, because:

- You may be entitled to an award in addition to any compensation you receive.
- You may be entitled to an award where you are not entitled to receive any compensation (for example, where your dismissal is not in breach of contract) or the real reason was that you were made redundant.

Do remember though, that if you decide to pursue a claim for an award, you must submit your claim to an industrial tribunal within three months of your employment being terminated, or six months where the reason is redundancy.

WHO CAN FIND OUT WHAT COMPENSATION I GET?

Anyone who obtains a copy of your company's financial statements.

The financial statements must disclose the total amount of any compensation paid to a director or past director for loss of office. This amount must include any payment you receive in respect of the loss of any other office you held. It will, therefore, include compensation for the loss of office as director, or as manager, of any subsidiary company. The amount should also include any compensation paid either while you were a director or immediately on your ceasing to be a director. However, the amount disclosed is the aggregate of compensation payments made in one year. So if more than one director receives compensation it is not possible to ascertain the amount paid to each director other than in the broadest terms.

In this context, 'compensation for the loss of office' includes *any* amount paid in connection with your retirement as a director. Because pensions are separately disclosed, they should not be included in this category of payment. Benefits in kind given to you on retirement, for example, your company car, may also have to be included. Alternatively, these may need to be disclosed as part of your 'emoluments' (see page 91). In fact, the statutory description of payments made as 'compensation for the loss of office' is widely drawn. In deciding whether a payment needs to be disclosed, you may need to take professional advice. Regard needs to be had both to the nature and circumstances of any payment rather than the description the company gives to it. For example, most *'ex gratia'* payments are *not* in fact regarded as gratuitous payments, but as payments in compensation for loss of office and therefore need to be disclosed.

MY COMPANY HAS TWO DIRECTORS. WE ARE THE ONLY SHAREHOLDERS. WHAT HAPPENS IF THE OTHER DIES?

You have a problem. Quite how serious it is depends on whether your company is private or public.

- Private companies

    Although the legislation permits a private company to have a sole director, most private companies adopt Table A as their Articles of Association. This provides that a company must have at least two directors, unless the company otherwise decides by ordinary resolution. In addition, the *quorum* required for the directors to transact business (see page 52) is two, unless the directors fix it at another number. Table A provides for the possibility of there being a sole continuing director. It says that he may act only to appoint another director(s) or call a general meeting of the company.

    So far so good. But consider the following example. In your company the directors are both shareholders. If one director/shareholder dies the company will only have one shareholder. The shares of the deceased shareholder will vest in his personal representatives, but depending upon whether the company's Articles of Association permit this, in a family company it may be undesirable to register the personal representative as a shareholder, since the personal representative will then be entitled to vote. Conversely, the personal representative may not seek to be registered as a shareholder and the company cannot compel him to. The *Companies Act 1985* provides that in such situations the remaining shareholder/director will be treated as if he were a sole trader – which he is in effect. If he carries on business for more than six months knowing that he is the only shareholder he will be liable personally for the company's debts during that period. Furthermore, to hold a general meeting there has to be a *quorum*, of two members.

You can imagine the problems that this type of situation can lead to. There can be no valid shareholders' meeting and the sole continuing director can only appoint another director or call a general meeting. This is a vicious circle. The only answer to this problem is to apply to the Secretary of State for Trade and Industry for a direction that the presence of one member can constitute a shareholders' meeting so that the meeting can appoint a new director. You are best advised to avoid this problem from the outset. The simplest method of doing so is to appoint a third director/shareholder, whose shareholding can be held as a nominee (see page 29).

- Public companies

The position outlined above applies equally to public companies with one difference. A public company must by law have at least two directors. Immediate action must, therefore, be taken if the number of directors falls below this. To quote from *Pennington's Company Law*:

> A sole director of a public company cannot act in its name or on its behalf in relation to outsiders, or even in relation to members (e.g. he cannot call general meetings or authorise the registration of share transfers). Outsiders who deal with a public company unaware that it has only one director may nevertheless be able to treat the company as bound by his acts . . .

12. DISQUALIFICATION

Page

So what's new? Haven't directors always been liable to be disqualified? 116

Does the legislation apply to all directors? 116

What can I be disqualified for? 117

What will the Court take into account in assessing whether I am 'unfit' to be a director? 119

That's a long list. Can I be disqualified for overlooking a minor statutory obligation? 120

Who decides whether I should be disqualified? 120

How long after an insolvency will it be before I know whether a summons will be issued against me? 121

How long can I be disqualified for? 121

What does disqualification mean? 122

What happens if I ignore the disqualification order? 123

Can I employ someone else to manage the company for me? 123

12. DISQUALIFICATION

Yes. For some years now a director has been liable to be disqualified in the following circumstances where:

- He is convicted of an indictable offence in connection with the promotion, formation, management or liquidation of a company.
- He appears to have been persistently in default regarding the statutory requirements in relation to returns, accounts and other documents required to be filed with the Registrar of Companies.
- He has been guilty in the course of the winding up of a company of fraudulent trading or some other fraud or breach of duty as officer, liquidator, receiver or manager of a company.
- He has been director of two or more companies that have gone into liquidation within five years and it appears to the Court that the director's conduct as director of any of those companies makes him unfit to be concerned in the management of a company.

The legislation, particularly in relation to the last two points, has been widened since 28 April 1986, and can now be found in the *Company Directors (Disqualification) Act 1986*.

Not only the fact that the scope of the law has widened should concern you as a director, but also that the DTI is more concerned that the law should be enforced. Seven disqualification orders were made under the new legislation within the first year of it coming into force. There were twenty such orders made in the same period relating to applications based on the old legislation. Although this may not sound a lot, the DTI had commenced proceedings against a further sixty directors by May 1987 with another six hundred cases under active consideration. Furthermore, the DTI has set itself targets of the numbers of directors it wants to see disqualified. So be alert to what follows in this chapter!

DOES THE LEGISLATION APPLY TO ALL DIRECTORS?

Yes. Any director may be disqualified if he satisfies any of the grounds for disqualification. The law expressly extends this to any person who occupies the position of a director, whatever title he is given (see

Chapter 2). Shadow directors may also be disqualified, but only on the grounds of 'unfitness' (see page 119).

You will, therefore, need to be aware of your responsibilities to avoid disqualification, even if, for example, you are a non-executive director or an alternate director, or even if you do not have the title of director at all, but are regarded as one by the law.

WHAT CAN I BE DISQUALIFIED FOR?

A director can be disqualified on three basic grounds – 'general misconduct in connection with companies', 'unfitness' and 'participation in wrongful trading' – as well as other miscellaneous grounds also mentioned below.

General misconduct in connection with companies

Broadly speaking this covers the existing grounds for disqualification prior to the new law. You can be disqualified:

- On conviction for certain indictable offences
  A director may be disqualified if he is convicted of an indictable offence in connection with the promotion, formation, management or liquidation of a company, or with the receivership or management of a company's property.
- For persistent breaches of the companies' legislation
  A director may be disqualified if he is persistently in default in filing any return, accounts or other document with the Registrar of Companies. This will be conclusively proven if he has been found guilty of three or more defaults in the five years ending with the date of the application.
- For committing fraud in the course of the winding up of a company
  A director may be disqualified if he appears to have been guilty of fraudulent trading (even if he has not been convicted for that), or has been guilty of any fraud or breach of duty in relation to his company.
- On summary conviction
  A director may be disqualified if he has been convicted of a summary offence after 15 June 1982 which relates to a breach of the companies' legislation requiring the filing of any return, accounts or other documents with the Registrar of Companies. This applies even where the breach is not one he has committed personally, but is committed by his company. However, to be disqualified he must

have been convicted of three or more defaults or had three or more default orders made against him.

Unfitness

The main change in the law is to permit the disqualification of directors for 'unfitness'. You must be particularly careful not to fall foul of this.

A director can be disqualified where he is (or has been) a director of a company that has at any time become insolvent and his conduct as director makes him unfit to be concerned in the management of a company. This applies even if the company becomes insolvent after he ceases to be a director of it. In fact, not only is a person's conduct as director of the company in question relevant, but also his conduct as a director of any other company or companies.

A company will be regarded as insolvent where either of the following applies:

- It goes into liquidation when it has insufficient assets to pay its debts, other liabilities and the winding up expenses.
- An administration order is made in respect of the company or an administrative receiver is appointed.

Participation in wrongful trading

This is a very important ground for disqualification, and you should refer to page 131 below, where a director's liability for fraudulent and wrongful trading is dealt with.

A court may disqualify a director from being a director whenever it makes an order that he should be personally liable for a company's debts because of fraudulent or wrongful trading, even if no application is made for this.

Other

- Undischarged bankrupts
  It is an offence for an undischarged bankrupt to act as a director of a company without the Court's permission. This extends to a director indirectly or directly taking part in or being concerned in the promotion, formation or management of a company.
- Failure to pay under a county court administration order.
- Disqualification after a company investigation.

WHAT WILL THE COURT TAKE INTO ACCOUNT IN ASSESSING WHETHER I AM 'UNFIT' TO BE A DIRECTOR?

The *Company Directors (Disqualification) Act 1986* sets out two lists of matters that a court must consider when it has to decide whether a person's conduct renders him unfit to be a director. The first list sets out those matters that apply regardless of whether the company is insolvent. The second sets out additional matters that apply where the company has become insolvent.

The first list requires the Court to consider:

- Any misfeasance or breach of any fiduciary or other duty by the director in relation to the company.
- Any misapplication or retention by the director of, or any conduct by the director giving rise to an obligation to account for, any money or other property of the company.
- The extent of the director's responsibility for the company entering into any transaction liable to be set aside as intended to defraud creditors.
- The extent of the director's responsibility for any failure by the company to comply with the *Companies Act 1985* provisions in respect of:

    - Accounting records.
    - The register of directors and secretaries.
    - The register of members.
    - The annual return.
    - The registration of charges.

- The extent of the director's responsibility for any failure by the directors of the company to comply with the duty to prepare annual accounts. This includes the provisions relating to the signing of the balance sheet and the documents to be annexed to it.

The second list requires the Court to consider:

- The extent of the director's responsibility for the causes of the company becoming insolvent.
- The extent of the director's responsibility for any failure by the company to supply any goods or services that have been paid for (in whole or in part).
- The extent of the director's responsibility for the company entering into any transaction or giving any preference that is liable to be set aside.

- The extent of the director's responsibility for any failure by the directors of the company to comply with the duty to call a creditors' meeting in a creditors' voluntary winding up.
- Any failure by the director to comply with the duties in relation to the company's statement of affairs, to deliver up company property to co-operate with a liquidator, and to attend the creditors' meeting in a creditors' voluntary winding up.

THAT'S A LONG LIST. CAN I BE DISQUALIFIED FOR OVERLOOKING A MINOR STATUTORY OBLIGATION?

Yes, in principle. However, the DTI in the Guideline Notes referred to below has stated that the 'office holder' (see below) should 'not take a pedantic view of isolated technical failures, e.g. the occasional lapse in filing annual returns, but should form an objective view of the director's conduct'.

WHO DECIDES WHETHER I SHOULD BE DISQUALIFIED?

Ultimately, it will be the Court that determines whether you should be disqualified. The procedure for this varies depending upon the grounds for disqualification in question.

General misconduct in connection with companies
An application for a disqualification order against a person for one of the grounds coming under this heading can be made by either:

- The Secretary of State for Trade and Industry or the Official Receiver.
- The liquidator, or any past or present member or creditor of any company in relation to which that person has committed an offence or other default.

Unfitness
A completely new procedure has been established in respect of the disqualification of directors for 'unfitness'.

Certain 'office holders' are now obliged to make reports on the conduct of directors and former directors to the Secretary of State for Trade and Industry where they consider the director's conduct makes him unfit. These 'office holders' are:

- The Official Receiver.
- A liquidator.
- An administrator.
- An administrative receiver.

Where the office holder takes the view that a particular director is, in his opinion, unfit to be a director, he must give details of the conduct that makes it appear that the conditions of the legislation are fulfilled, as above. Furthermore, in submitting these reports, the office holder must have regard to the DTI Guideline Notes – *Disqualification of Directors – Completion of Statutory Report and Returns.*

Where a report is made, the Secretary of State may decide to make an application (or direct the Official Receiver to do so) to the Court for a disqualification order.

Furthermore, in all situations, the office holder must make an interim report within six months of appointment to the effect that he has not submitted the above report either because he is not aware of any matters that would require him to make a report or because sufficient information is not to hand. However, the fact that such a report is submitted does not preclude a report subsequently being made should any relevant information become available.

Participation in wrongful trading

No formal application is necessary for a disqualification order in these situations. The Court that is considering the issue of fraudulent or wrongful trading will also consider whether to make a disqualification order.

HOW LONG AFTER AN INSOLVENCY WILL IT BE BEFORE I KNOW WHETHER A SUMMONS WILL BE ISSUED AGAINST ME?

The Secretary of State for Trade and Industry has two years from the commencement of insolvency to decide whether or not to apply for a disqualification order.

HOW LONG CAN I BE DISQUALIFIED FOR?

This will depend upon the reason for the disqualification. The period will be one of the following:

- Maximum of five years

- Disqualification on summary conviction for certain indictable offences in connection with the promotion, formation, management or liquidation of the company.
- Disqualification for persistent breaches of the companies' legislation.
- Disqualification on summary conviction in contravention, or failure to comply with company legislation covering the filing of returns, etc.

- Maximum of fifteen years
  - Disqualification on trial on indictment for certain indictable offences.
  - Disqualification for committing fraud in the course of the winding up of a company.
  - Disqualification for participation in wrongful trading.
  - Disqualification after the investigation of a company.

- Minimum of two years, maximum of fifteen years
  - Disqualification where a company has become insolvent and the conduct of the director makes him unfit.

In all these situations the actual period of disqualification ordered will depend on all the circumstances of the case.

WHAT DOES DISQUALIFICATION MEAN?

If a disqualification order is made against a person it means that he must not for the period specified in the order, without the leave of the Court, be:

- A company director.
- A liquidator or administrator of a company.
- A receiver or manager of a company's property.
- In any way, directly or indirectly, concerned in or take part in, the promotion, formation or management of a company.

The final heading can be quite wide. The Courts have held that acting as a management consultant advising on the financial management and restructuring of a company may constitute being directly or indirectly concerned in the management of a company.

WHAT HAPPENS IF I IGNORE THE DISQUALIFICATION ORDER?

First of all, if a person breaks a disqualification order, or the provisions relating to undischarged bankrupts, he is liable to either:

- Imprisonment for up to two years and/or an unlimited fine, on conviction on indictment.
- Imprisonment for up to six months and/or a fine not exceeding £2,000, on summary conviction.

Secondly, he will be personally liable for all the 'relevant debts' of a company if at any time he breaks a disqualification order, or the provisions relating to undischarged bankrupts, by being involved in the management of a company. The 'relevant debts' of a company are those debts and other liabilities incurred while he was involved in its management.

The law regards a person as being involved in the management of a company not just if he is a director of it, but also where he is concerned directly or indirectly, or takes part in, its management.

CAN I EMPLOY SOMEONE ELSE TO MANAGE THE COMPANY FOR ME?

Yes, but any person who is involved in the management of a company (defined as above) and acts, or is willing to act on your instructions, without obtaining permission from a court, will also be personally liable for all the 'relevant debts' of the company. In this context, 'relevant debts' are those debts and other liabilities incurred by the company while that person acts or is willing to act on your instructions. And in addition, once a person has acted on your instructions in this way, the law will treat him as willing to do so from then on, unless he can actually prove that he is not willing to. Furthermore, you would almost certainly be a shadow director of the company yourself in these circumstances (see page 30), and similarly liable.

13. COMPANY INVESTIGATIONS

Page

When can the Department of Trade and Industry investigate my
company?... 125

What are the consequences of an investigation? 126

13. COMPANY INVESTIGATIONS

WHEN CAN THE DEPARTMENT OF TRADE AND INDUSTRY INVESTIGATE MY COMPANY?

The Secretary of State for Trade and Industry has extensive powers to appoint an inspector to investigate and report on a company's affairs, its control and share dealings in it. The appointment of an inspector is a very serious matter and tends to be restricted to large public companies. The circumstances leading to appointment are often the subject of rumour and speculation and so the public announcement of an appointment is rarely a complete surprise. The inspectors appointed for an investigation are usually a senior partner in a firm of chartered accountants and a lawyer (either senior counsel or a senior partner in a firm of solicitors). The DTI is willing to provide the inspectors with the administrative facilities they may need, although frequently these will be provided by the inspectors' own firms.

There are obviously circumstances where the matters of complaint regarding a company are not public knowledge and it is best for them to remain so until the facts are ascertained. On such occasions, the Secretary of State may take advantage of his power to order an inspection of the company's books and papers. The inspection will invariably be carried out by officers of the DTI and will be discreet.

You can find out more general information about company investigations from the *Handbook of the Companies Inspection System* (HMSO).

There are three situations in which an inspector may be appointed to carry out an investigation:

- To investigate a company's affairs
  The Secretary of State can appoint an inspector if he considers that one of the following applies:

    - The company has been formed for a fraudulent or illegal purpose.
    - The company has been run so as to defraud creditors, for some other fraudulent or unlawful purpose, or in a manner that is unfairly prejudicial to shareholders.
    - Those who formed or manage the company have been found guilty of fraud, misfeasance or other misconduct towards the company or its shareholders.
    - The company's shareholders have not been given all the

information that they would reasonably expect about the company's affairs.

The Secretary of State must appoint an inspector if a court orders that a company is to be investigated. Furthermore, the Secretary of State *may* appoint an inspector where 200 or more shareholders, or holders of one tenth of the company's issued share capital, apply for an investigation. Such applications are not common. First, the applicant must be able to show that he has a good reason for requiring the investigation and may be required to support this with evidence. Secondly, the applicant may be required to pay up to £5,000 security in advance of an investigation and *all* the costs subsequently.

- To investigate the ownership or control of your company
  Where 200 or more shareholders or holders of one tenth of the company's issued share capital apply, the Secretary of State may appoint an inspector to determine 'the true persons who are or have been financially interested in the success or failure (real or apparent) of the company or able to control or materially influence its policy'. The Secretary of State *cannot* refuse to order an investigation unless the application is vexatious, or refuse to investigate any particular matter unless it is unreasonable. The cost of any such an application is borne by the Secretary of State.
- To investigate share dealings
  The Secretary of State may appoint an inspector to investigate any circumstances that suggest to him that unlawful share dealings may have occurred. For example, such share dealings may include a director dealing in options in his company's shares or failing to notify his company that he has an interest in its shares (see page 104).

WHAT ARE THE CONSEQUENCES OF AN INVESTIGATION?

The final product of the inspectors' investigation will obviously be their written report. This has traditionally taken some time to be published (where published).

There may be the following consequences for a director:

- If the investigation reveals that a director has committed a criminal offence (for example, the destruction or falsification of any document relating to your company's affairs) you may be prosecuted.

- The Secretary of State can apply to the High Court for a disqualification order (see page 121) against you where he considers that this is expedient in the public interest.

There may be the following consequences for the company concerned:

- The Secretary of State, if he considers it expedient in the public interest, can present a petition for the company to be wound up if the Court finds that that is just and equitable.
- The Secretary of State can bring civil proceedings in the name of any company (for example, for the recovery of a company's property) where he considers that they ought to be brought in the public interest.
- Where the Secretary of State considers that the affairs of a company have been conducted in a manner that is unfairly prejudicial to shareholders, he may make a petition on this ground to the High Court. The High Court can then make a wide variety of orders, for example to 'regulate the conduct of the company's affairs in the future'.

14. FINANCIAL DIFFICULTIES AND COMPANY INSOLVENCY

Page

I think that my company is in financial difficulties. What should I do? 129

What alternatives are open to my company? 129

Can I just keep on trading? 130

What about an injection of capital? 132

Could I do a deal with my creditors? 132

How can my company be reconstructed or amalgamated? 132

What is an 'administration order'? 133

What does an 'administrator' do? 133

What will happen to me as a director when an administrator is appointed? 134

What is meant by 'receivership'? 134

What will happen to me as a director when a receiver is appointed? 135

What is meant by 'voluntary winding up'? 136

What is meant by 'compulsory winding up'? 137

I've received a letter from the Registrar of Companies, saying that my company is about to be struck off the register. What does this mean? 139

14. FINANCIAL DIFFICULTIES AND COMPANY INSOLVENCY

I THINK THAT MY COMPANY IS IN FINANCIAL DIFFICULTIES. WHAT SHOULD I DO?

You and your co-directors must seek and obtain independent professional advice. In the first instance, your auditors should be able to help you. In practice, unless the financial difficulties have arisen suddenly, they will be aware of your situation as they carry out their review of your financial position as part of their normal auditing procedures. Depending upon their advice, you may decide to contact a 'licensed insolvency practitioner' who specialises in receiverships or liquidations. For professional reasons, the 'licensed insolvency practitioner' you consult, if he is to accept appointment as office holder, may ultimately need to be from a different firm than your auditors.

It is also important that you contact your company's bankers and keep them well informed of the situation. Frequently, financial difficulties arise because of temporary cash flow problems. However, a well presented case to the bank, supported by your professional advisors, may enable you to obtain an increased loan facility.

Depending upon the circumstances, it may be advisable for your creditors to be contacted to defer payment of outstanding accounts.

Although this chapter is entitled 'Financial difficulties and company insolvency', your professional advisors' first aim will be to formulate some kind of rescue plan, if that is possible, and preserve the company, or a substantial part of it, in its existing form. Although in many situations this is possible, it is very important for you to remember that if there is a real risk that the company might become insolvent, leaving creditors unpaid, and if you continue to trade and incur debts, you may later be held personally liable for those debts.

WHAT ALTERNATIVES ARE OPEN TO MY COMPANY?

First, before any informed decision can be made about the company's future, you are likely to be advised to ensure that the accounting records are up to date and regular management accounts are prepared. Frequently, when companies experience financial difficulties, administrative factors are neglected in favour of what happens at the 'sharp end'. One of the first considerations, if the company is experiencing cash flow problems, will be to produce short term profit forecasts and cash flow projections. In the long term, it may be necessary to ascertain the parts of a business's activities that are profitable and those that are not (possibly with a view to 'hiving off' the profitable parts). All possibilities will require that your professional advisors have the financial data they need to help you make an informed decision.

Secondly, it may be that, after investigating the financial position of your company thoroughly, you conclude that it is insolvent and cannot trade its way out of the situation. There are many options open to you. It is not practicable to give more than an outline of these here, but you may find the following of assistance in understanding the proposals that might be put forward by your professional advisors. Some of these options are commercial in nature, others relate to the procedures established for insolvent companies by law. Not all of these relate to the winding up of a company. The law has been sweepingly revised in the *Insolvency Act 1986* and it is hoped that the procedures established there will provide the framework in which ailing companies can survive. The order in which your options are laid out commences with those which will least affect your company and end with the compulsory termination of your company's life. The options are:

- An injection of capital into your company (see page 132).
- Arrangements with your company's creditors (see page 132).
- The reconstruction or amalgamation of your company (see page 132).
- An 'administration order' (see page 133).
- Receivership (see page 134).
- Voluntary winding up (see page 136).
- Compulsory winding up (see page 137).

CAN I JUST KEEP ON TRADING?

This will depend upon your circumstances as outlined above. The law provides four principal sanctions against directors who act irresponsibly with regard to their creditors.

- Criminal liability for fraudulent trading
  Any person who has been knowingly party to a company's fraudulent trading may at any time (regardless of whether the company ever goes into receivership, administration or liquidation) be prosecuted for this as a criminal offence. 'Fraudulent trading' here means carrying on the business of a company with intent to defraud its (or any other person's) creditors or for any other

fraudulent purpose. This is a serious offence. On trial or indictment the penalties are a maximum of seven years imprisonment and/or an unlimited fine, or on summary trial a maximum of six month's imprisonment and/or a fine of up to £2,000. However, the offence of fraudulent trading is notoriously difficult to prove and has been largely superseded by the wrongful trading provisions (see below).

- Personal liability for fraudulent trading

  Any person who has been knowingly party to a company's fraudulent trading may be made liable by the Court to contribute to the company's assets, but *only* when it is in the course of winding up. As with the criminal offence of fraudulent trading, this has been for all practical purposes superseded by the wrongful trading provisions (see below).

- Personal liability for wrongful trading

  If a company goes into an insolvent liquidation, a person who knew (or ought to have concluded) that there was no reasonable prospect that the company would avoid going into insolvent liquidation *before* winding up commenced, and who was a director of the company at the time, may be made liable by the Court to contribute to the company's assets. In contrast to the position with fraudulent trading, a person can be liable for wrongful trading even if his intentions were not dishonest in any way. Accordingly, the law provides that a person cannot be liable for wrongful trading if the Court is satisfied that after that person became aware that there was no reasonable prospect that the company could avoid an insolvent liquidation, he took every step with a view to minimising the potential loss to the company's creditors that he ought to have taken.

  When considering what facts a person 'ought' to have known or found out, the 'conclusions' he ought to have reached and the 'steps' which he ought to have taken, the Court will compare them with those of a 'reasonably diligent person'. The 'reasonably diligent person' is assumed to have the general knowledge, skill and experience expected of a person entrusted with or carrying out the same functions as the director in question as well as the general knowledge, skill and experience that the director in question actually has. This has the effect, therefore, of placing a higher duty upon you if you possess a special skill, for example, if you are a Finance Director and a chartered accountant, or if you are a Company Secretary and a solicitor.

- Disqualification
  A person who is responsible for fraudulent or wrongful trading may
  be disqualified (see page 117).

WHAT ABOUT AN INJECTION OF CAPITAL?

Very often a company finds itself in difficulties because of cash flow
problems even though, technically, it is quite solvent. In such
circumstances the answer may be to obtain external finance. The terms
upon which such capital is received should be considered in close
consultation with your professional advisors. For example, will the
provider of the capital want to take an equity share in your company?

COULD I DO A DEAL WITH MY CREDITORS?

Again, where a company's financial difficulties stem from temporary
cash flow difficulties, one answer may be for it to come to an
arrangement of some sort with its creditors. There are various ways to
achieve this from informal arrangements to defer payment on the one
hand to legally binding arrangements under the supervision of an
insolvency practitioner on the other.

HOW CAN MY COMPANY BE RECONSTRUCTED OR AMALGAMATED?

The concepts of reconstruction and amalgamation are highly technical
in legal terms.

A reconstruction or amalgamation can be proposed between a
company and its creditors or between a company and its members. To
reconstruct your present company it will be dissolved, yet its business
will survive by being transferred to a new company set up for this
purpose. The new company will have an improved capital structure or
other advantages that will leave it solvent.

A similar process is common during receivership and is known as
'hiving down'. What happens is that the receiver sells the assets under
his control to a new company set up for the purpose. The shares in the
new company are then held by nominees of the receiver in trust for the
old company. The advantage of this procedure is that the new company
can be sold more easily.

An amalgamation of your company takes place where your company
merges with another.

WHAT IS AN 'ADMINISTRATION ORDER'?

As noted above, you may be liable for wrongful trading unless you can show that you have taken every step with a view to minimising the potential loss to your company's creditors. One way that you can do this is to seek the appointment of an 'administrator'. In fact, your company's shareholders and creditors can also do this.

An administrator, who must be a qualified insolvency practitioner, acts in a similar way to the traditional receiver (see page 134) of a company who is usually appointed by a bank to manage a business until a debenture is repaid. In fact, it was the success of that procedure that has led to the introduction of the administration procedure, that can operate where there is no debenture holder to appoint a receiver.

An administration order appointing an administrator can be obtained by presenting a petition to the Court. You must satisfy the Court that the company is, or is likely to become, unable to pay its debts, but is not in liquidation. The Court can only make an order if it considers it likely to achieve one or more of the following purposes:

- The survival of the company, and the whole or any part of the business, as a going concern.
- The approval of a voluntary arrangement with creditors (see page 136).
- The sanctioning of a company reconstruction.
- Compromise or settlement with creditors, not being a reconstruction.
- A more advantageous realisation of the company's assets than there would be if the company was wound up.

WHAT DOES AN ADMINISTRATOR DO?

An administrator must prepare proposals that show how the purposes specified in the administration order can be achieved. A formal statement of these must be made to the Court within three months. In practice, commercial reasons dictate a shorter period. This statement has to be given to the company's shareholders, creditors, and the Registrar of Companies. A meeting of creditors must be called to consider the proposals. If they are approved, the administrator will be required to manage the affairs, business and property of the company in accordance with those proposals. To do this he is given power to 'do all such things as may be necessary for the management of the affairs, business and property of the company'. A long list of particular powers is given in the Act.

WHAT WILL HAPPEN TO ME AS A DIRECTOR WHEN AN ADMINISTRATOR IS APPOINTED?

You will remain a director, although you can only exercise your powers in such a way that will not interfere with the administrator. You may be dismissed by the administrator. The administrator can also appoint directors. The administrator must report on any unfit director to the Secretary of State for Trade and Industry, and this may result in a disqualification order being made (see page 120). When the administrator has achieved his purposes he must apply for a court order to discharge him. If you are still a director, unless the company is wound up, you will then be able to exercise all your powers as you did before the order was made.

WHAT IS MEANT BY 'RECEIVERSHIP'?

Frequently, when a company appears to be in financial difficulties (and often otherwise) a major creditor, usually the company's bank, will continue to trade with the company only on the condition that the company gives security for the balance owing to it. The document in which this security will be given is called a 'debenture' or 'debenture deed'. The most common type of debenture creates what is called a 'floating charge'. It 'floats' in that it is a charge on both the present and future assets of your company, whatever they may be. The debenture deed specifies particular events, such as default on repayment of a loan, that will terminate your permission to deal with the assets subject to the charge and entitle the debenture holder to appoint a receiver. This is called the 'crystallisation' of the charge. The other type of charge is a 'fixed charge' that relates to specified assets only, such as your company's land and buildings.

A debenture will usually entitle its holder to the appointment of a receiver in the following circumstances:

- Where your company fails to repay the monies secured by the debenture.
- Where your company exceeds its debenture trust deed's borrowing limits and does not comply with notices requiring a reduction in borrowing.

- Other breaches of the debenture deed.
- At the request of the directors.

The receiver (called an 'administrative receiver' in the case of a floating charge) must be a qualified insolvency practitioner. A person appointed purely under a fixed charge is merely called a 'receiver' and, surprisingly, does not need to be a qualified insolvency practitioner. He is appointed as an individual even though he may be a partner in, for example, a firm of chartered accountants.

The purpose of an administrative receiver's appointment is for him to take control of the charged assets with a view to paying off the liability to the debenture holder, although he must pay off any 'preferential debts' first. In this situation where a receiver is appointed, the company is not in 'receivership'. However, a company is in receivership where an administrative receiver is appointed.

WHAT WILL HAPPEN TO ME AS A DIRECTOR WHEN A RECEIVER IS APPOINTED?

You will be in a very similar position to that where an administrator is appointed (see page 134), although depending upon the terms of the debenture your powers may be less restricted. Most important of all, as soon as a receiver is appointed you will no longer have the authority to deal with the property charged under the debenture. Where there is a floating charge this will effectively divest you of any real authority within your company. In contrast to the position where an administrator is appointed, however, a receiver does not have the power to dismiss you as a director.

You must remember, however, that although you are divested of many of your powers as a director, you are still subject to the same obligations as before, for example, to file an annual return with the Registrar of Companies.

Like an administrator, a receiver is under a duty to report on any unfit director to the Secretary of State for Trade and Industry, which may result in a disqualification order being made (see page 120).

Frequently, receivership leads towards a company's liquidation (see page 136). However, if a receiver is able to pay off the debenture you will continue to be a director with full powers as before.

WHAT IS MEANT BY 'VOLUNTARY WINDING UP'?

If your company is in financial difficulties, yet is solvent in that it could pay its debts in full by selling its assets, it may be advantageous to consider a voluntary winding up. An orderly winding up will invariably realise a higher value for assets than a forced sale.

A voluntary winding up is commenced when the shareholders of a company adopt a resolution for their company to be wound up. The principal types of voluntary winding up are known as either a 'members' voluntary winding up' or a 'creditors' voluntary winding up'. The liquidation will proceed as a members' voluntary winding up provided that a majority of the board of directors make a statutory declaration of the company's solvency within five weeks before the adoption of the winding up resolution. Otherwise the winding up will have to proceed as a creditors' voluntary winding up.

The statutory declaration has to state that the directors making it have made a full enquiry into the affairs of the company and have formed the opinion that the company will be able to pay its debts in full, together with interest, within a specified period that must not exceed twelve months from the commencement of the winding up. The statutory declaration must include a statement of the company's assets and liabilities at the latest practicable date before it is made. As a director, you should consider very carefully whether or not to make such a declaration. If the company's debts are not paid or provided for within the period stated those who made the statement will be presumed by the law *not* to have had reasonable grounds for making it. Further, any director who makes the statutory declaration without having reasonable grounds for the opinion expressed in it, commits a criminal offence. This is punishable with imprisonment for up to two years and/or an unlimited fine on trial or indictment or to a maximum of six months imprisonment and/or a fine of a maximum of £2,000 on summary trial.

The shareholders will usually appoint a liquidator at the general meeting at which the winding up resolution is adopted. No notice is required to propose the appointment. This is important, because until a liquidator is appointed after the resolution the directors commit an offence if they continue to exercise their powers. The appointment of a liquidator will usually bring your powers to an end as a director, although the shareholders or the liquidator may permit you to exercise some or all of your powers.

The liquidator will act to realise all the company's assets and distribute the proceeds to creditors and shareholders, subject to his own costs. If at any time he comes to the opinion that the company will not be able to pay its debts in full within the stated period, he must call a meeting of the company's creditors and the winding up will become a creditors' voluntary winding up.

If a creditors' voluntary winding up comes about for one of the reasons above, there are certain consequences. The liquidator must hold a creditors' meeting that will decide whether to appoint a liquidator in place of himself, because he was appointed by the shareholders. There are various publicity requirements that attempt to ensure that creditors are aware of the opportunity to exercise their votes. At the creditors' meeting the creditors may decide to appoint a liquidation committee to assist the liquidator and to receive reports on the progress of the liquidation.

The procedure for the final dissolution of the company, once the liquidator has realised the company's assets and completed the necessary distribution, is considered on page 139.

WHAT IS MEANT BY 'COMPULSORY WINDING UP'?

The meaning of 'winding up' has been considered above in the context of voluntary winding up. Those persons who may present a petition before a court seeking the compulsory winding up of a company are:

- The company.
- The company's directors.
- The Secretary of State for Trade and Industry.
- A contributory (usually meaning a shareholder).
- A creditor.
- An official receiver (for companies only registered in England Wales, as there is no official receiver in Scotland).
- An administrative receiver, administrator or supervisor.

The grounds on which a petition may be sought are as follows:

- The company has passed a special resolution that it be wound up by the Court.
- It is a public company and a year or more has expired without it obtaining a certificate relating to compliance with its share capital requirements (see page 11).
- The company does not commence business within a year of its incorporation or suspends business for a year.

- The number of shareholders is reduced below two (see page 86).
- The company is unable to pay its debts. This is the most common ground where a creditor petitions for a company's winding up. A company is deemed to be unable to pay its debts primarily where a creditor owed more than £750 has served a written demand on a prescribed form requiring the company to pay the sum due and the company fails to pay it within three weeks.
- The Court considers it just and equitable that the company should be wound up. This ground is often used in small companies, that are essentially a partnership in corporate form, where there is an irrecoverable difference of opinion between the 'partners'.

The procedure for a compulsory winding up usually commences when a creditor presents a petition to the County Court (where the company's paid up share capital does not exceed £120,000) or to the Chancery Division of the High Court. A copy of the petition is served at the company's registered office and a date will be fixed for the petition to be heard. There are various publicity requirements and, in addition, the creditor has to file an affidavit with the Court. A 'provisional liquidator' may be appointed before the petition is heard to preserve the company's assets. This effectively takes away the directors' powers, although they retain a power to apply to the Court to discharge the order. For obvious reasons, the application has to be made *ex parte*, which means that the company will not have an opportunity to put its side of the case. It would be unfair if such an order could be made without the company having any redress, and so the Court will invariably require an undertaking from the petitioner that he will compensate the company for any loss it suffers if winding up is not subsequently ordered.

On the assumption that the petition is granted by the Court, the Official Receiver will be appointed as provisional liquidator to take custody of the company's assets. The Official Receiver is appointed by the Secretary of State for Trade and Industry and each court in England and Wales which has jurisdiction in insolvency has one or more Official Receivers attached to it. Their main task is to investigate the causes of insolvencies and to act as a liquidator in compulsory liquidations. Within twelve weeks of the winding up order the Official Receiver may call separate meetings of creditors and contributories to decide whether an application should be made to the Court for someone other than the Official Receiver to be appointed as the liquidator. Alternatively, the Official Receiver may apply himself to the Secretary of State for Trade and Industry to appoint a liquidator.

There are various publicity requirements in respect of those meetings.

Insolvency practitioners, usually acting as part of a firm of chartered accountants, will generally only accept appointment as liquidator where a company has sufficient assets to pay their fees. However, most will be willing to attend creditors' meeting on behalf of creditors free of charge in the hope that they will be appointed liquidator. Where a company has few assets, it will not usually be worthwhile appointing a liquidator (if one could be found willing to be appointed) and the Official Receiver will act as liquidator. This occurs in the majority of cases.

In contrast to the position in a voluntary winding up, the law does not expressly provide that your powers as a director cease on the appointment of a liquidator. However, the extensive powers of a liquidator will leave you with little role. For example, the liquidator is under a duty to take into his custody or control all the company's property.

The law places a duty on a number of persons, including the company's officers, directors, company secretary and auditor to give the liquidator such information concerning the company as he reasonably requires and also to attend upon him at such times as he may reasonably require. You cannot escape this by resigning, it applies to those who have been officers of the company at any time. Employees are also under this obligation. It is a criminal offence to fail to comply.

When the liquidator has realised all the company's assets and completed the distributions necessary he will send a summary of receipts and payments to the creditors and contributories with a notice that he intends to apply for his release. He will then send a final account to the DTI. The liquidator must summon a final creditors' meeting when it appears to him that the winding up is complete for all practical purposes. He then notifies the Registrar of Companies that the final meeting has been held. On receipt of that notice the Registrar of Companies must complete various publicity requirements and after three months the company will be dissolved.

I'VE RECEIVED A LETTER FROM THE REGISTRAR OF COMPANIES, SAYING THAT MY COMPANY IS ABOUT TO BE STRUCK OFF THE REGISTER. WHAT DOES THIS MEAN?

This is probably not the first letter you have received from the Registrar of Companies! It probably means that you have not filed an annual return or some other document required by the *Companies Act 1985* for some time and have ignored various reminders.

The procedure for striking companies off the register works in the following way. If the Registrar of Companies has reasonable cause to believe that a company is not carrying on business (for example, because it fails to file any documents or reply to correspondence) he will write to the company enquiring whether it is in operation. If he receives no reply to this he sends a warning letter, such as you have received. If you do not reply to this he will issue a notice in the London Gazette (in the case of a company registered in England and Wales) and send you a copy. The notice will state that the company will be struck off the register (unless a reason is shown for it not to be) three months from the date of the notice. If your company has been struck off the register by this procedure, it can be restored. However, you should seek professional advice on how to achieve this.

APPENDICES

Page

I   Table of Requirements for a Company's Statutory Books ... 142

II   PRO NED Code of Recommended Practice on Non-Executive Directors 144

III   Table of Criminal Offences that Directors and other Officers may be convicted of 146

IV   Directors' Loans Decision Tables 156

APPENDIX I

TABLE OF REQUIREMENTS FOR A COMPANY'S STATUTORY BOOKS

Register or book	Companies Act 1985 reference	Where to be kept	Whether available for public inspection
Register of Interests in Shares (public companies only)	S.211	With Register of Directors' Interests in Shares and Debentures	Yes
Register of Directors and Secretaries	SS.288 to 290	At Registered Office	Yes
Register of Directors' Interests in Shares and Debentures	S.325	At Registered Office or with Register of Members	Yes
Register of Members	SS.352 to 353	At Registered Office or some other place (if within the country in which the company is registered and is notified to the Registrar of Companies)	Yes
Minutes of shareholders', directors' and managers' meetings	SS.382 to 383	At Registered Office (shareholders' meetings)	No, but shareholders may inspect minutes of shareholders' meetings
		Where directors decide (directors' and managers' meetings)	No

Register or book	Companies Act 1985 reference	Where to be kept	Whether available for public inspection
Register of Charges	SS.406 to 407	At Registered Office	Yes
Directors' service contracts	S.318	At Registered Office, with the Register of Members or the company's principal place of business (if within the country in which the company is registered)	No, but shareholders may inspect
Accounting records	SS.221 to 222	Where directors decide	No

APPENDIX II

PRO NED CODE OF RECOMMENDED PRACTICE ON
NON-EXECUTIVE DIRECTORS

1. Effective Boards are essential to the success of British business. In quoted companies, Boards are more likely to be fully effective if they are comprised both of able Executive Directors and strong, independent Non-Executive Directors.

2. For the purposes of this Code, an independent Non-Executive Director is one who has the integrity, independence, personality and experience to fulfil the role of the Non-Executive Director effectively. Independence is more likely to be assured when the Non-Executive Director:

   (a) Has not been employed in an executive capacity by the company on whose Board he or she sits, within the last five years:

   (b) If a professional adviser, is not retained by the company (whether personally or through his or her firm) on a continuing or regular basis: and

   (c) Is not (whether personally or through his or her employer) a significant customer of or supplier to the company.

3. In larger quoted companies where the turnover is £50 million or more or whose employees number 1000 or more, the Board should normally include at least three independent Non-Executive Directors; and independent Non-Executive Directors (including the Chairman, if he or she meets the criteria in Clause 2) should comprise about one-third of the Board. In smaller quoted companies, or in larger companies which have small Boards, the provisions of this Code should be followed in a manner and to an extent appropriate to the size of the Board and commensurate with the company's resources.

4. The main tasks of the Non-Executive Directors are to contribute an independent view to the Board's deliberations; to help the Board provide the company with effective leadership; to ensure the continuing effectiveness of the Executive Directors and management; and to ensure high standards of financial probity on the part of the company. If they are to succeed in these tasks the Non-Executive Directors will need to enjoy the full support of the Chairman, and will need to be provided with the information which in their view they require in order to carry out their duties. They will also need to receive such information in sufficiently good time to enable them to give it their proper consideration.

5. The Non-Executive Directors should be consulted on major issues of audit and control. Their task will be facilitated by the establishment of an Audit Committee whose functions should be to consider important financial information, the adequacy of systems of financial control, the scope of the audit and the auditors' remuneration; and to put recommendations on these matters to the Board. The committee should be composed mainly or wholly of Non-Executive Directors, and its chairmanship and quorum should reflect this: the Non-Executive Directors on it should have the right to see the auditors alone if they wish.

6. The Board's most important functions include:

(a) The appointment, dismissal and remuneration of top executive management:

(b) The appointment and dismissal of Directors to or from executive positions, especially that of Chief Executive: and

(c) The appointment and remuneration of all Directors.

The execution of these functions will be facilitated if an Appointments and Remuneration Committee is established, the majority of whose members are Non-Executive Directors.

7. Non-Executive Directors should normally be appointed on the understanding that they are joining the Board for a specific term, subject to re-election by rotation in the usual way. After the expiry of this term, renewal should not be considered to be automatic by either party.

8. Companies which do not at present comply with the provisions of this Code should aim to implement the necessary changes within a reasonable period of time.

April 1987

PRO NED
10 Gough Square,
London EC4A 3LR.
Telephone 01-583 8033

APPENDIX III

TABLE OF CRIMINAL OFFENCES THAT
DIRECTORS AND OTHER OFFICERS MAY BE CONVICTED OF

The table below summarises only the criminal offences contained in the Companies Act 1985 that both directors and other officers may be convicted of. There are, however, many other offences that a company may have to face that have consequences for directors and other officers. A full list of offences under the Companies Act is contained in Schedule 22 of the Companies Act 1985. Of course, directors and other officers may also be liable for criminal offences committed under other Acts of Parliament and these are not dealt with here.

1 THE COMPANIES ACT 1985

Section of Act creating offence	General nature of offence	Mode of prosecution	Punishment	Daily default fine (where applicable)
80(9)	Directors exercising company's power of allotment without the authority required by Section 80(1).	1. On indictment 2. Summary	Unlimited fine £2,000	
88(5)	Officer of company failing to deliver return of allotments, etc., to Registrar.	1. On indictment 2. Summary	Unlimited fine £2,000	£200

Section of Act creating offence	General nature of offence	Mode of prosecution	Punishment	Daily default fine (where applicable)
95(6)	Knowingly or recklessly authorising or permitting misleading, false or deceptive material in statement by directors under Section 95(5).	1. On indictment 2. Summary	2 years or unlimited fine, or both. 6 months or £2,000 or both.	
111(3)	Officer of company failing to deliver copy of asset valuation report to Registrar.	1. On indictment 2. Summary	Unlimited fine £2,000	£200
141	Officer of company concealing name of creditor entitled to object to reduction of capital, or wilfully misrepresenting nature or amount of debt or claim, etc.	1. On indictment 2. Summary	Unlimited fine £2,000	
142(2)	Director authorising or permitting non-compliance with Section 142 (requirement to convene company meeting to consider serious loss of capital).	1. On indictment 2. Summary	Unlimited fine £2,000	
156(7)	Director making statutory declaration under Section 155, without having reasonable grounds.	1. On indictment 2. Summary	2 years or unlimited fine, or both. 6 months or £2,000 or both.	

147

Section of Act creating offence	General nature of offence	Mode of prosecution	Punishment	Daily default fine (where applicable)
169(6)	Default by company's officer in delivery to Registrar of the return required by Section 169.	1. On indictment	Unlimited fine	£200
		2. Summary	£2,000	
173(6)	Director making statutory declaration under Section 173 without having reasonable grounds for the opinion expressed in the declaration.	1. On indictment	2 years or unlimited fine, or both.	
		2. Summary	6 months or £2,000, or both.	
223(1)	Company failing to keep accounting records (liability of officers).	1. On indictment	2 years or unlimited fine, or both.	
		2. Summary	6 months or £2,000, or both.	
223(2)	Officer of company failing to secure compliance with, or intentionally causing default under, Section 222(4) (preservation of accounting records for requisite number of years).	1. On indictment	2 years or unlimited fine, or both.	
		2. Summary	6 months or £2,000, or both.	
231(4)	Default by director or officer of a company in giving notice of matters relating to himself for purposes of Schedule 5 Part V.	Summary	£400	

Section of Act creating offence	General nature of offence	Mode of prosecution	Punishment	Daily default fine (where applicable)
235(7)	Non-compliance with the section, as to directors' report and its content; directors individually liable.	1. On indictment 2. Summary	Unlimited fine £2,000	
238(2)	Laying or delivery of unsigned balance sheet; circulating copies of balance sheet without signatures.	Summary	£400	
240(5)	Failing to send company balance sheet, directors' report and auditors' report to those entitled to receive them.	1. On indictment 2. Summary	Unlimited fine £2,000	
243(1)	Director in default as regards duty to lay and deliver company accounts.	Summary	£2,000	£200
245(1)	Company's individual accounts not in conformity with requirements of this Act; directors individually liable.	1. On indictment 2. Summary	Unlimited fine £2,000	
245(2)	Holding company's group accounts not in conformity with Sections 229 and 230 and other requirements of this Act; directors individually liable.	1. On indictment 2. Summary	Unlimited fine £2,000	

Section of Act creating offence	General nature of offence	Mode of prosecution	Punishment	Daily default fine (where applicable)
254(6)	Company or officer in default contravening Section 254 as regards publication of full individual or group accounts.	Summary	£400	
255(5)	Company or officer in default contravening Section 255 as regards publication of abridged accounts.	Summary	£400	
260(3)	Director of special category company failing to secure compliance with special disclosure provision.	1. On indictment 2. Summary	Unlimited fine £2,000	
288(4)	Default in complying with Section 288 (keeping register of directors and secretaries, refusal of inspection).	Summary	£2,000	£200
291(5)	Acting as director of a company without having the requisite share qualification.	Summary	£400	£40
294(3)	Director failing to give notice of his attaining retirement age; acting as director under appointment invalid due to his attaining it.	Summary	£400	£40

Section of Act creating offence	General nature of offence	Mode of prosecution	Punishment	Daily default fine (where applicable)
305(3)	Company default in complying with Section 305 (directors' names to appear on company correspondence, etc.).	Summary	£400	
306(4)	Failure to state that liability of proposed director or manager is unlimited; failure to give notice of that fact to person accepting office.	1. On indictment 2. Summary	Unlimited fine £2,000	
314(3)	Director failing to comply with Section 314 (duty to disclose compensation payable on takeover, etc.); a person's failure to include required particulars in a notice he has to give of such matters.	Summary	£400	
317(7)	Director failing to disclose interest in contract.	1. On indictment 2. Summary	Unlimited fine £2,000	

Section of Act creating offence	General nature of offence	Mode of prosecution	Punishment	Daily default fine (where applicable)
318(8)	Company default in complying with Section 318(1) or (5) (directors' service contracts to be open to inspection); 14 days' default in complying with Section 318(4) (notice to Registrar as to where copies of contracts and memoranda are kept); refusal of inspection required under Section 318(7).	Summary	£400	£40
323(2)	Director dealing in options to buy or sell company's listed shares or debentures.	1. On indictment 2. Summary	2 years or unlimited fine, or both. 6 months or £2,000, or both.	
324(7)	Director failing to notify interest in company's shares; making false statement in purported notification.	1. On indictment 2. Summary	2 years or unlimited fine, or both. 6 months or £2,000, or both.	
326(2),(3) (4),(5)	Various defaults in connection with company register of directors' interests.	Summary	£400	Except in the case of section 326(5) £40

Section of Act creating offence	General nature of offence	Mode of prosecution	Punishment	Daily default fine (where applicable)
328(6)	Director failing to notify company that members of his family have, or have exercised, options to buy shares or debentures; making false statement in purported notification.	1. On indictment 2. Summary	2 years or unlimited fine, or both. 6 months or £2,000, or both.	
329(3)	Company failing to notify Stock Exchange of acquisition of its securities by a director.	Summary	£400	£40
342(2)	Relevant company entering into transaction or arrangement for a director in contravention of Section 330.	1. On indictment 2. Summary	2 years or unlimited fine, or both. 6 months or £2,000, or both.	
342(3)	Procuring a relevant company to enter into transaction or arrangement known to be contrary to Section 330.	1. On indictment 2. Summary	2 years or unlimited fine, or both. 6 months or £2,000, or both.	
343(8)	Company failing to maintain register of transactions, etc. made with and for directors and not disclosed in company accounts; failing to make register available at Registered Office or at company meeting.	1. On indictment 2. Summary	Unlimited fine £2,000	

Section of Act creating offence	General nature of offence	Mode of prosecution	Punishment	Daily default fine (where applicable)
349(3)	Officer of company issuing business letter or document not bearing company's name.	Summary	£400	
349(4)	Officer of company signing cheque, bill of exchange, etc. on which company's name not mentioned.	Summary	£400	
350(2)	Officer of company, etc., using company seal without name engraved on it.	Summary	£400	
351(5)(b)	Officer or agent of company issuing, or authorising issue of, business document not complying with those subsections.	Summary	£400	
391(4)	Directors failing to convene meeting requisitioned by resigning auditors.	1. On indictment 2. Summary	Unlimited fine £2,000	
408(3)	Officer of company refusing inspection of charging instrument, or of register of charges.	Summary	£400	£40
426(7)	Director or trustee for debenture holders failing to give notice to company of matters necessary for purposes of Section 426.	Summary	£400	

Section of Act creating offence	General nature of offence	Mode of prosecution	Punishment	Daily default fine (where applicable)
450	Destroying or mutilating company documents; falsifying such documents or making false entries; parting with such documents or altering them or making omissions.	1. On indictment 2. Summary	7 years or unlimited fine, or both. 6 months or £2,000, or both.	
451	Making false statement or explanation in purported compliance with Section 447.	1. On indictment 2. Summary	2 years or unlimited fine, or both. 6 months or £2,000, or both.	
458	Being a party to carrying on company's business with intent to defraud creditors, or for any fraudulent purpose.	1. On indictment 2. Summary	7 years or unlimited fine, or both. 6 months or £2,000, or both.	

APPENDIX IV

DIRECTORS' LOANS DECISION TABLES

Decision table 1: Loans – relevant company

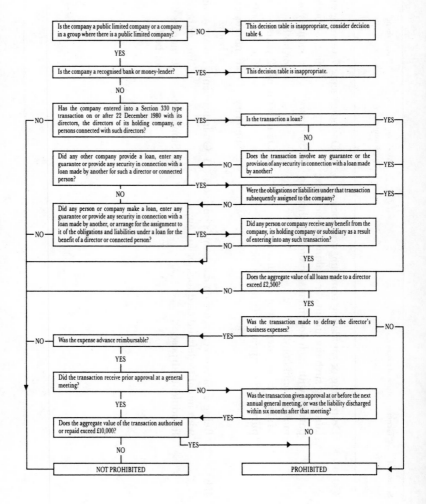

Decision table 2: Quasi-loans – relevant company

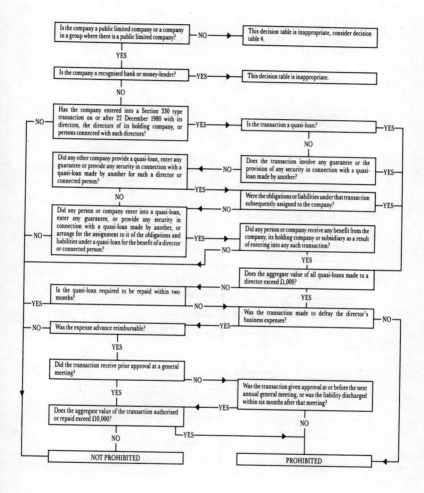

Decision table 3: Credit transactions – relevant company

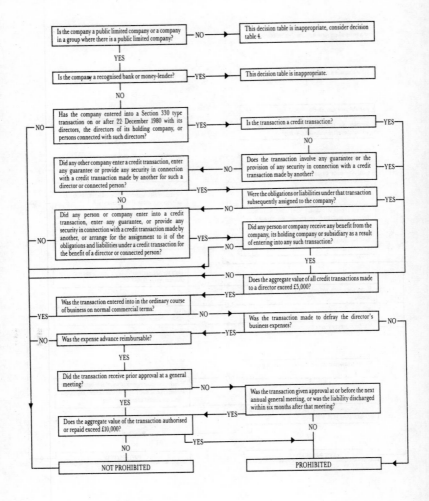

Decision table 4: Loans – non-relevant company

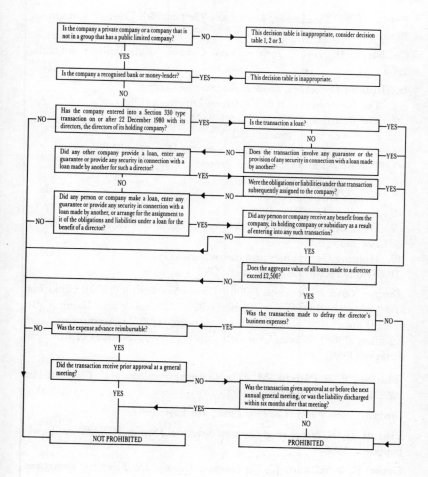

BIBLIOGRAPHY

Franks, J.A., *The Company Director and The Law,* 5th Edition, Longman, 1986.

Goldstein, B., *How to Form a Private Company,* 30th Edition, Jordans, 1985.

Institute of Directors, *Guide to Boardroom Practice:*
1. The Remuneration of Executive Directors (1986)
2. The Board and the Auditors (1984)
3. Employee Involvement (1987)
4. Share Ownership for Employees and Directors (1986)
5. The Board and Consumer Protection (1984)
6. Directors' Personal Liabilities (1984)
7. Insider Dealing (1986)
8. Nominee Directors (1985)
9. Directors and Financial Management following the Insolvency Act 1985 (1986)
10. Holding Companies and Subsidiaries (1986)
11. The Director's Appointment (1987)

Directors' Guide to: Pensions (1986), Direct Marketing (1986), Choosing and Using an Advertising Agency (1985), Choosing and Using a PR Consultancy (1985), Company Insurance (1985), Accounting and Auditing (1986), Screen Communications (1986), Sources of Business Finance (1986).

Johnson, B. & Patient, M., *The Accounting Provisions of the Companies Act 1985,* Farringdon, 1985.

Jordans, *Form Finder. Company Forms,* Jordans, 1987.

Lintott, G.D., *Handbook of Company Secretarial Practice,* ICSA/Woodhead-Faulkner, 1986.

Loose, P. & Yelland, J., *The Company Director: His Functions, Powers and Duties,* 6th Edition, IOD/Jordans, 1987.

Mills, G., *On the Board,* Allen and Unwin, 1985.

Roberts, D., *The Administration of Company Meetings,* ICSA/Woodhead-Faulkner, 1986.

Roberts, D., *How to Form a Company,* 2nd Edition, ICSA/Woodhead-Faulkner, 1986.

Ryan, C.L., *Company Directors: Liabilities, Rights and Duties,* 2nd Edition, CCH Editions, 1987.

Scrine, A.J., *Be your own Company Secretary,* ICAEW/Kogan Page, 1987.

Sealy, L.S., *Disqualification and Personal Liability of Directors,* 2nd Edition, CCH Editions, 1987.

Smith, C.G.S., *Company Procedures Manual,* Longman, 1987.

Souster, P., *The Responsible Director,* ICAEW, 1987.

Tricker, R., *The Independent Director,* Tolleys, 1978.

Walmsely, K., *Company Secretarial Practice: Manual of ICSA,* ICSA/Woodhead-Faulkner, 1984.

Wright, D., *Rights and Duties of Directors,* Butterworths, 1987.

INDEX

Page

Accounting records..73-79
disqualification for failure to keep,.........................76
meaning, ...73
retention of, ...75

Accounts
auditors. See *Auditors*
definition of, ...77
directors' report, ...20
disclosure in. See *Disclosure*

Administrator – See *Insolvency*

Alternate director 28-29
appointment, ...29

Annual General Meeting – See *General Meeting*

Annual return 77-78, 117-119

Appointment
auditor, of, ...17-18
chairman, of, ...54
company secretary, of,.......................................15-16
director, of. See *Appointment of director*
solicitor, of,...21

Appointment of director – See also *Disqualification, Eligibility*............32-33
managing director,...41
over age of 70, where, ...24
specific powers in articles as to, ...7

Articles of Association 6
powers of directors in, ...7
remuneration of directors under,.............................90
vacation of office under the, ...109

162

	Page
Auditor	15,17-21
audit, explanation of,	19-21
appointment of,	17-18
independence,	18
removal of,	19
remuneration of,	18
report,	19-21
Board – See also *Board meetings*	52-59
chairman of,	54
delegation of powers,	38
dismissal of director by,	111
Board meetings – See also *Board*	52-59
agenda of,	54-55
directors' duty to attend,	55
exclusion of director from,	56
minutes of,	57-59
notice of,	53
quorum at,	52
Breach of duty	119
Capital	5,132
requirement of a public company,	4,11,25
Certificate of Incorporation	5,10,11
Chairman	54
disclosure of emoluments,	92
Cheques	39
Common law duties of directors	
company, to,	43
duty of care,	43
employees, to,	44
fidicuary duty,	44
indemnity in respect of,	49
insurance in respect of,	49

Page

Companies..2-22
different types of,..10-12

Company forms 4-5,22

Company seal 10

Company secretary 15-17

Compensation 111-13

Contract 45,49
interest of director in, ...45
personal liability of director on, ...38-39
of service,...33-35,82
ultra vires, ...5
void,..47

Correspondence
directors' names on, ...35-36

Creditors..132
arrangements with, in financial difficulties,...............132
defrauding of, ...130
meeting of,...137

Credit transaction 47-49,96-101

Department of Trade and Industry Investigations 125-127

Directors
accounting responsibilities of. See *Accounting records, Accounts*
age limit of, ...24
alternate. See *Alternate director*
another company of, as director, ...27

Page

appointment of. See *Appointment of Director*

board meetings. See *Board meetings*

common law duties of. See *Common law duties of directors*

competition with company,...49

connected persons of,...93

contracts with company, ...45

disclosure of interests, requirements as to. See *Disclosure*

dismissal of. See *Dismissal of director*

disqualification of. See *Disqualification of director*

eligibility, ...24,27,28

employee, as,..33

family of. See *Directors, connected persons of*

fiduciary duty of. See *Fiduciary duty*

first, appointment of, ...4

formal objection where disagreement with board, ...58

indemnity of, ...49

insider dealing. See *Insider dealing*

insolvent companies of. See *Insolvency*

interests of –

    disclosure of. See *Disclosure*

    register of. See *Register of Director's Interests in Shares and Debentures*

loans to. See *Loans to directors*

managing. See *Managing director*

meetings, disqualification when absent from, ...55-56

nominee. See *Nominee director*

non-executive. See *Non-executive director*

personal liability of. See *Personal liability of directors*

powers of. See *Powers of directors*

qualifications of. See *Directors, eligibility*

re-election of retiring, ...24

register of. See *Register of Directors and Secretaries.*

relatives of. See *Directors, connected persons of*

remuneration. See *Remuneration of directors*

resignation of. See *Resignation of director*

retirement of. See *Retirement of director*

shadow. See *Shadow director*

share dealings of. See *Share dealing*

shareholders, relationship with. See *Meetings, Shareholders*

speak at general meetings, right to, ...85

spouse of. See *Directors, connected persons of*

Page

Disclosure
annual return, of, ...78
charges, register of. See *Register of Charges*
conflicts of interest, and, ...27,45
directors and secretaries, register of. See *Register of Directors and*
    Secretaries
documents available for inspection, ...12,75
interest − 45-46
loans to directors of − 48,92-101
material interest in contract − 45-49,98-101
names of directors' on company correspondence, ...35-36
remuneration of directors', in accounts, of, ...91
service contracts, directors', available for inspection, ...34-35

Dismissal of director − See also *Disqualification of director* 110-113

Disqualification of director − See also *Dismissal of director* 13,116-123

Dividends 78-79

Duties of directors − See *Directors, duties of*

Eligibility − See *Directors, eligibility*

Employee 61-71
contract of employment, ...63-64
discrimination on grounds of sex, race or disability, ...61-62,68-69
dismissal of − 69-71
distinguished from the self-employed, ...61
duties of directors to, ...44
employer's liability insurance, ...65
foreign employees, ...69
health and safety of, ...67
itemised pay statements, ...64
pay as you earn (PAYE), ...64-65
payments, ...65
holidays, ...66
pregnancy, ...66
sickness, ...65-66
recruitment of, ...61-62
references, ...63
trade unions and, ...67

Page

Extraordinary general meeting – See also *General meeting* 82-83

Extraordinary resolution 88

Fiduciary duty 44

Financial statements – See *Accounting records*

Formation of company 4-5

Fraudulent trading 130-132
disqualification of director for, ...117-123
meaning of, ...130-131
personal liability of director for, ...131
wrongful trading and, compared, ...131

General meeting 81-88
annual accounts laid before. 81
annual general meeting. 81
auditors – See *Auditors*
chairman at, ...85
directors' right to attend, ...85
extraordinary general meeting. See *Extraordinary general meeting*
notice of. See *Notice, general meeting*
quorum at, ...86
resolutions at. See *Resolutions*

Insider dealing 105-106
Company Securities (Insider Dealing) Act 1985, ...13,105
criminal offence, as, ...107

Insolvency 13,129-140
administrative receiver, ...135
administrator, ...133-134
compulsory winding up, ...137-140
disqualification of director and. See *Disqualification of director*
fraudulent trading. See *Fraudulent trading*
minimise potential loss to creditors, directors duty to, ...131
misfeasance, ...119
personal liability of directors in. See *Personal liability of directors*
practitioners 129,132
voluntary winding up, ...136-137
wrongful trading, ...131-132
personal liability of directors. See *Personal liability of directors*
receivership reconstruction and amalgamation 132

Page

Investigations – See *Department of Trade and Industry Investigations*

Liquidation – See *Insolvency, Winding up*

Loans to directors 48,92-101
business expenditure, ...95-96
credit transactions 96
   definition of, ...96
   minor, ...96-100
definition of loan, ...94
expenses for, ...95
indirect arrangements, prohibition on, ...97
material interest in 98-101
penalties for contravention, ...101
quasi-loan 96
   definition of, ...96
   short term, ...96
small loans 93,100

Managing Director 41

Meetings
board. See *Board meetings*
general. See *General meetings*

Memorandum of Association 5

Mental disorder 24

Minor 24

Minutes 8,57-59

Misfeasance 119

Names 9
company, change of, ...9
directors', on company correspondence, ...35
trading, ...9

Nominee director 29-30

Non-executive directors 31-32
function of, ...32
PRO NED, ...31

	Page
Notice	53
board meetings, of,	53
general meetings, of,	83
special,	83
Office holder – See also *Insolvency*	120
Officer – See also *Directors, Company Secretary, Auditors*	14-15
Ordinary resolution – See *Resolution*	
Personal liability of directors	2,12,49,131-132
cheques, on,	39
contracts, on,	38-39
fraudulent trading and,	13,117,119,121-122
managing director and,	41
wrongful trading and,	131
Powers of directors – See also *Directors*	38-41
articles of association, in,	6
outside company's objects as to,	5
Private companies – See *Companies, different types of*	
Property	
substantial transactions involving directors,	46-47
Public Companies – See *Companies, different types of*	
Qualification of directors – See *Directors, eligibility*	
Receivership – See *Insolvency*	
Records	
accounting. See *Accounting records*	
directors' service contracts. See *Disclosure, service contracts*	
register of charges. See *Register of charges*	
register of debenture holders. See *Register of debenture holders*	
register of directors and secretaries. See *Register of directors and secretaries*	
retention of, by companies,	75
statutory books,	7-8,16
Registered office	5,8
Register of charges	8

Page

Register of debenture holders 8

Register of directors and secretaries...32,33

Register of directors' interests in shares and debentures 7,104-105

Registrar of Companies 8,21-22

Removal of directors – See *Directors, Dismissal of director, Disqualification of director*

Remuneration of directors 90-101

Resignation of director 109

Resolution..83-84
extraordinary,...88
ordinary – 17,86
   appoint auditor other than retiring auditor, to, ...19
   appoint director over age of 70, to,...................................24
special,...83,87

Retirement of director 110

Service contracts directors' 33-35
annual general meeting and,...35
available for inspection, ...35,82
compensation under, where director dismissed, ...34
exempted from disclosure,...35
not to exceed five years,...35
remuneration under, ...34

Shadow directors 30

Share dealings 103-107
Department of Trade and Industry, investigation of,............125-127
disclosure of interests by directors, ...103-104
insider dealing,..105
register of directors' interests in shares and debentures. See *Register of directors' interests in shares and debentures*

Shares..4,5,11
dealings in. See *Share dealings*
directors' interest in. See *Disclosure*

Page

Shareholders – See also *General meeting, share dealings* 14

Special resolution – See *Resolutions*

Stock Exchange 3,11,32,33,47-49,82,105
Yellow Book, generally,...47

Table A – See *Articles of Association*

Transactions 47-49
loans to directors. See *Loans to directors*
substantial property. See *Property, substantial transactions involving directors*

Ultra vires 5

Unfitness...118-120

Unlimited Companies – See *Companies*

Winding up – See *Insolvency*

Wrongful trading – See *Insolvency*

Yellow Book – See *Stock Exchange*

THE INSTITUTE OF DIRECTORS

The Institute of Directors represents almost 35,000 business leaders in the UK and overseas. Membership is individual, and directors of public and private companies, partners and professional men and women of all disciplines are eligible to join. The IOD aims to encourage and assist its members to improve their professional competence as business leaders, to provide an effective voice, to represent the interests of its members and to bring the experience of the business leader to bear on the conduct of public affairs for the common good.

The IOD is developing its role as a professional body to assist directors in carrying out the increasingly complex nature of their task. Through courses, conferences and publications the Institute is establishing itself as the authority on the role, structure and conduct of company boards and on the responsibilities of directors in the UK and thus contributes towards an improvement in the standards of business leadership. The IOD is advised by specialist committees which ensure that the best possible experience and professional advice is available in drawing up authoritative guidance on best practice in company direction and to ensure effective self-regulation.

The Institute of Directors has an established close working relationship with Ministers and senior civil servants in key departments in Whitehall and maintains regular contact with the Members of the House of Commons and House of Lords. It represents the view of directors to government and promotes the skills, standards of conduct and economic and social contribution of directors and other business leaders.

The Institute invites membership enquiries from all newly-appointed directors at its Pall Mall offices. Please contact the Marketing Department, Institute of Directors, 116 Pall Mall, London SW1Y 5ED. Tel: 01-839 1233, Fax: 01-930 1949, Telex: 21614 IOD.

DELOITTE HASKINS & SELLS
OFFICES IN THE BRITISH ISLES

Aberdeen
6 Golden Square,
Aberdeen AB9 1JB.
Telephone: (0224) 636555

Belfast
Northern Bank House,
10 High Street,
Belfast BT1 2BL.
Telephone: (0232) 246969

Birmingham
35 Newhall Street,
Birmingham B3 3DX.
Telephone: 021-200 2828

Bristol
Bull Wharf,
Redcliff Street,
Bristol BS99 7TR.
Telephone: (0272) 260514

Cambridge
Mount Pleasant House,
Huntingdon Road,
Cambridge CB3 0BL.
Telephone: (0223) 314992

Cardiff
Tudor House, 16 Cathedral Road,
Cardiff CF1 6PN.
Telephone: (0222) 239944

Croydon
Melrose House,
42 Dingwall Road,
Croydon CR0 2NE.
Telephone: 01-681 5252

Edinburgh
P.O. Box 90,
25 Abercromby Place,
Edinburgh EH3 6QS.
Telephone: 031-557 3333

Glasgow
100 Wellington Street,
Glasgow G2 6DJ.
Telephone: 041-248 7932

Gloucester
Lennox House,
Beaufort Buildings,
Spa Road, Gloucester GL1 1XD.
Telephone: (0452) 423031

Leeds
Cloth Hall Court, Infirmary Street,
Leeds LS1 2HT.
Telephone: (0532) 455166

Liverpool
Richmond House,
1 Rumford Place,
Liverpool L3 2HT.
Telephone: 051-227 4242

London
P.O. Box 207,
128 Queen Victoria Street,
London EC4P 4JX.
Telephone: 01-248 3913

P.O. Box 198,
Hillgate House,
26 Old Bailey,
London EC4M 7PL.
Telephone: 01-248 3913

Manchester
Bank House,
Charlotte Street,
Manchester M1 4BX.
Telephone: 061-236 9565

Newcastle upon Tyne
Hadrian House, Higham Place,
Newcastle upon Tyne NE1 8BP.
Telephone: 091-261 2121

Norwich
7 Queen Street,
Norwich NR2 4ST.
Telephone: (0603) 624181

Nottingham
Compass House,
The Ropewalk,
Nottingham NG1 5DQ.
Telephone: (0602) 419066

Reading
P.O. Box 147,
Venture House,
37/43 Blagrave Street,
Reading RG1 1RY.
Telephone: (0734) 596711

Southampton
Wheatsheaf House,
24 Bernard Street,
Southampton SO9 1QL.
Telephone: (0703) 634521

Swansea
P.O. Box 60,
Midland Bank Chambers,
Castle Square SA1 1DU.
Telephone: (0792) 475777

Channel Islands
Whitely Chambers,
Don Street,
St. Helier, Jersey, C.I.
Telephone: (0534) 75151

Albert House, South Esplanade,
St. Peter Port, Guernsey, C.I.
Telephone: (0481) 728278

Republic of Ireland
43-49 Mespil Road,
Dublin 4
Telephone: (0001) 604400/605500

European Communities Office
Avenue de Cortenberg 79/81,
Boite 7, B1040, Brussels.
Telephone: 02 736 2058